W/D

SOp

Silver Galore

The mysterious southern belle, Careen Langridge, has come West to escape death threats from fanatical Confederates. Is she still being pursued? Should she marry Captain Robbie Randall? But the Mexican, Aristide Luna, has other plans. With gambler and fast-gun, Luke Short, he murders Randall's men and targets Careen.

Can the amiable cowboy, Tex Anderson and his pal, Pancho, impose rough justice as with guns blazing they go to Careen's aid?

Silver Galore

John Dyson

A Black Horse Western

ROBERT HALE · LONDON

© John Dyson 2007
First published in Great Britain 2007

ISBN 978-0-7090-8335-1

Robert Hale Limited
Clerkenwell House
Clerkenwell Green
London EC1R 0HT

Typeset by
Derek Doyle & Associates, Shaw Heath
Printed and bound in Great Britain by
Antony Rowe Limited, Wiltshire

ONE

'A stampede! That's what they call it.' Eighteen-year-old Lucille Langridge surveyed the throng of new arrivals pouring into Oro City, families in covered wagons, bearded miners and their mules, city dudes, gambling men and speculators, and a clutch of screaming girls jumping down from the overloaded stagecoach amid a maze of half-erected cabins and store fronts. 'That's just what it looks like, too.'

'I guess it's all good for business,' Careen, her sister, older by ten years or so, replied, as they tried to make their way along the crowded wooden side-walk. 'The more men there are, the less likely it is they'll be happy with their lot.'

Their father ran the town gunshop and Careen's comment implied a rise in their sales of weapons and bullets. 'I don't think that's nice,' Lucille sang out. 'You sound as if you'd be happy to see them start shooting at each other.'

'Grow up, child,' Careen replied. 'I'm a realist. Wherever there's gold or silver there's bound to be trouble. Mankind's natural greed.'

Silver, it seemed, there was in plenty. Prospectors had been sniffing around these gulches high in Colorado's Rocky Mountains since before the Big War. Abe Lee had struck it rich in a stream named California Gulch and in 1860 there'd been a rip-roaring gold rush to this very spot. But the gold had fizzled out, the miners had moved on, and Oro City had almost become a ghost town for thirteen years. Now, in 1877, it looked like it was all starting again.

'What on earth do all these girls plan to do?' Lucille asked, as they made way for the bunch of saucy creatures off the stagecoach who sashayed past and pushed into a saloon. 'There surely aren't enough jobs for them serving in the stores.'

'Darling, don't ask.' Careen wondered just how naïve her sister could be. Admittedly, Lucille was still young, but, by her age, Careen had seen more than enough of the world's wicked way in the war. 'I wouldn't care to explain.'

'You don't mean. . . ?' Lucille's eyes widened with curiosity. 'I wondered why they were wearing those silk dresses and feathered hats, so much rouge.'

It might be early summer but it was still chill up here in the mountains at an altitude of 10,000 feet. Blizzards would be as likely to sweep down from the icy peaks about them in mid-June as in winter snows. So the gunmaker's daughters were attired

6

more sensibly in warm homespun dresses, sunbonnets, boots and woollen shawls.

The Langridges, themselves, had abandoned their once magnificent Memphis home as soon as the war ended, crossing the Mississippi and heading out by prairie schooner across the plains. Droughts, tornadoes, snowstorms, marauding Sioux, on they had trudged. They had paused awhile in Denver City, the mining town on the eastern slopes of the Central Divide that rose suddenly from the plains like a great wall. But Jim Langridge had loaded up his wagon and pushed on, climbing up through the tortuous gorges and across windy passes until he reached Oro City. Only then, amid that straggle of houses and forgotten stores, the neglected mine shafts along the gulch, did he feel safe.

What a difference today! What a babble of tongues: Mexicans, Poles, Italians, Irish, Hebrews. Honest stampeders, and dishonest drifters. Tradesmen setting up shop: dentists, lawyers, carpenters, timber merchants, cigar sellers, fortune-tellers, tattooists, boarding-house-keepers, meat and game butchers, horse dealers, gamblers, publicans, all aiming to sift some of the miners' riches. Dudes in tophats and cutaway coats rubbed shoulders with dirty old desert rats in coonskin caps and tattered buckskins.

Even now a dozen pair of oxen were stood morosely in the knee-deep muck as their double wagonload of whiskey barrels was rolled down

7

ramps and into the saloons and brothels, some still just tents.

The more solidly constructed general merchandise store of Horace Tabor had been the centre of what commerce there was in the area for several years. The sisters pushed into its murky interior redolent of apple barrels and leather saddles and greeted the flint-faced Augusta Tabor.

'Good morning, girls,' she squawked. 'What will it be?'

Lucille produced their shopping list which the dour New Englander inspected through her pince-nez. Her prow of purple nose protruded from a face made more gaunt by hair scraped back into a bun. The Tabors had been out West since '57 and, by working her fingers to the bone, it was largely due to Augusta's efforts that they had prospered.

Her walrus-moustached husband, Horace, was more inclined to take his ease over in the saloon. He had been doing so, involved in a game of poker the previous year when two ancient German prospectors, with little more than a pick, bucket, shovel and an old faithful dog between them, had begged him to grubstake them for one last try in the hills.

Tired by their importuning Tabor had given them $17 of supplies in return for one third of their earnings, if any, and got back to his game. He was more surprised than anybody when they returned one day to say they had sunk a shaft twenty-seven

8

feet deep that appeared to have hit a thick vein of silver running straight down into the hillside. Horace was still playing poker but now he had a gigantic diamond ring on his finger and a thousand dollars a week pocket money.

'How's the mine going?' Careen could not resist asking.

Mrs Tabor, the town's only official post-mistress and banker up until that time, fixed her with her glacial eyes and frowned. 'I don't like it. It's too much wealth for any one body to handle. I wish it had never been found. No good will come of it. I fear it's sending Horace crazy. He's spending cash like there's no tomorrow, investing in all kinds of crazy schemes.'

'He was buffoonish enough to begin with,' Careen whispered to Lucille as they left the store, 'but I certainly wouldn't be so fussed if I had a husband likely to become a millionaire.'

Two hicks tumbled out of The Timbuctoo saloon and tried to paw them as they passed. 'Come an' jine us, sweetheart,' one drawled.

'Get your filthy hands off me,' Careen countered, slashing viciously at them with her parasol, then clip-clopped on her way in the high-heeled riding boots she wore beneath her ankle-length grey dress.

Maybe they mistakenly figured the girls for fallen doves, but the Langridge sisters were two of a small number of virtuous females in Oro. Although, if truth be known, in Careen's case it hadn't always been so. At twenty-nine she was still a handsome young woman in a more mature and curvy way than her slim sister. To the men who watched her pass her air of mystery had great allure. Once Careen had been the belle of many a Memphis ball, but that was all long in the past.

Lucille wrinkled her pert nose as they passed an open sewer. And to avoid a dead mule in which rats had made their nest she hoisted her skirts and plunged across the main street, the mud sucking at her boots. 'Holy cow!' she exclaimed. 'Why doesn't somebody do something about cleaning up this town?'

Men, however, were too busy boring into the adjacent hillsides or, if they struck lucky, spending their dust in the saloons and cat-houses to worry about the possibility of an outbreak of typhus.

'Mr Tabor's more interested in building an opera house,' Careen cried, as she climbed on to the opposite sidewalk to her father's shop. 'James Langridge, gunmaker and repairer', it was announced above the door.

'Come on,' she said, 'from now on there'll be plenty of work for us, too, you'll see.'

TWO

Captain Robert Randall stood outside the entrance to the Skinned Alive Mine and felt reasonably pleased with the ore taken out so far. Packed into tarpaulin panniers it was being loaded by his seven labourers on to mules, ready for transportation down to Oro City.

'What do you think, Hal?' he asked his engineer. 'You figure we're on to something?'

'Of course we are.' The portly Harold Callaghan, a derby perched on his head, and wrapped in a long duster coat, dipped his hand into one of the panniers. 'This grey carbonate of lead sludge may not look much to you, but it might well yield two-and-a-half pounds of silver to the ton. Same as Horace is bringing out.'

Randall, a tall, broad-shouldered man of military bearing, was attired in a faded topcoat over a roll-neck jersey, riding breeches, and stout boots. He still wore his comfortable, wide-brimmed cavalry

11

hat, with the crossed swords insignia, but was no longer in the army. However, like many ex-officers he kept his title, and parts of his uniform.

'Well,' he grunted, jerking the pannier knots tight and checking the *aparejos* of the mules. 'Looks like we've come up trumps. Fingers crossed! At least I should have enough to pay the boys' wages.'

'You'll have more than that,' Callaghan beamed. 'Much more. You can count on it. This is just the start.'

Randall had been a twenty-year man, latterly aide-de-camp to General Crook, chasing Apaches through the length and breadth of Arizona Territory. His time served with distinction, he decided not to re-enlist as the previous summer the Third Cavalry marched north to join a punitive expedition against the Sioux. This culminated in Custer leading 224 brave men of the Seventh, plus a newspaper reporter, to their deaths.

Instead, Randall headed for the Rockies at the time Horace Tabor hit it rich. Surveying that same stretch of the Mosquito Range he made an educated guess that the deep vein of silver might well run northwards. There was an old Spanish mine in the vicinity, long since abandoned. But silver had been found there in former times. So the ex-captain of cavalry consulted mining engineer Callaghan. Yes, they agreed, it was worth giving it a go, but they would need to dig much deeper.

Skinned Alive Creek was a woeful name but it had

been called such by mountain men after one of
their number had suffered this fate at the hands of
Utes after he had ravished one of their maidens. So
Randall registered his claim in that name at Denver.

'OK, let's get going,' he shouted and swung on to
an ex-army plug, Rajah, who, like him, had served
his time honourably. He raised his hand and led his
men, each leading a loaded mule, down the steep-
sided defile through the mountains, Callaghan
bringing up the rear.

Aristide Luna knelt amid precipitous rocks sharp as
razors, his rifle hugged into his shoulder, and
peered down into Skinned Alive Creek. Deep in the
shadow of the still snow-streaked slopes he had spotted the mule train descending. He guessed they
were loaded with much valuable silver ore.

The Mexican's dark-hued face had the alertness of
a hawk watching its prey. He turned and signalled
with his rifle to two *vaqueros* perched on the rim of the
far side of the canyon. 'Get ready, *amigos*,' he hissed
more to himself. 'These thieves will not get far today.'

The creek was well-named and today it would
know more bloodshed. Luna thumbed back the
side hammer of the .55 calibre Springfield, lining
up the sights of the forty-inch barrel on Captain
Randall's chest. Amid the silence of the mountains
the only sound was that of the mules' bells ringing
out mournfully. '*Sí*,' Aristide muttered. 'The bells
toll for your funeral.'

13

But suddenly Callaghan hollered, 'Hold it, men. One of them panniers is slipping. We better fix it.' And, as luck had it, the mule train came to a halt.

'The devil take them!' the Mexican hissed in Spanish, for Randall had slipped from his horse and disappeared from his sight on the far side of the mules as he went back to attend to the apparatus. 'Never mind, the fat one will do,' he said. Maybe he was the more important. Without his expertise the Skinned Alive would grind to a halt.

Luna adjusted his sights, lining them up on Callaghan's ruddy, cheerful countenance as he sat his horse. 'You have chosen your own fate,' he muttered. 'You die first.'

'Which one?' Randall asked, as he reached his engineer.

'This one in front of me.' Harold pointed to it and chuckled. 'Now we've stopped I may as well have a sup.' He took a silver flask from his coat, unscrewed the top and raised it to his lips.

'You and your brandy. There's nothing wrong with that *aparejo*. In my opinion this is just a ruse so you can have a break.'

'Ah!' Callaghan sighed with satisfaction as he swallowed. 'A man's gotta keep his insides warm. How abou—'

The word was never finished. Callaghan's cheery face was smashed apart in a mess of splintered bone and blood. He was sent tumbling from his bay to hit the rocks.

Captain Randall saw his stricken face as he heard the whining snarl of the bullet followed by the echo of the rifle report bouncing off the canyon walls. 'Hell!' Stunned, he ducked under the bay's eye-bulging head and took a look at the engineer. Dead. Dead as the proverbial dodo. 'Good God!'

Simultaneously two more rifle shots clapped out. But they came from the other side of the canyon, the slugs whistling and ricocheting off the rocks. 'Keep your heads down, men!' Randall hollered. 'They're trying to kill us all.'

He caught hold of the shuddering bay before it panicked the mules, dragged it into the lee of the cliff and hitched it to a pine bough. It occured to him that under such an ambush of triaxial firing their chances were slim of getting out alive. Especially as he was the only one with a carbine, but that was in Rajah's saddle boot. He had better get along to him before he, too, panicked and set off.

More shots were barking out and one of the mules bared its teeth in a scream as blood fountained from its chest and it crashed to one side on its load.

'Hot damn!' Anger surged through the ex-captain and disregarding his own safety he dodged away as fast as he could along the line to Rajah. The big old horse was alarmed but well trained, and waited until his master had snatched his Spencer carbine from the boot and was given a slap to go on his way into safety. 'Now,' Randall said, peering up over the rocks. 'Where is that first shootist?' Not only did the man up there appear to be the better marksman, but Randall wanted revenge for his shot friend.

'Can you see him, sir?' His foreman, Aaron Rooney, wriggled up alongside him. He pointed upwards to where black powdersmoke drifted. 'I saw his big sombrero. A greaser by the look of him.'

With expertise born of many years of battle Randall fired upwards at the whereabouts of the killer, but ducked back for some kind of cover as a shower of bullets from all sides chipped rock fragments and toppled a pine bough on to their heads. 'They've certainly got us pinned down,' the mine-owner stated, as he tried to struggle free to another position and reload. One of the crew gave a yelp of pain as he, too, was hit. 'I'll somehow have to try to get out of here and work my way up.'

'No, sir,' Rooney pleaded. 'I wouldn't. I don't go much on your chances if you do – the chances of any of us.'

'Bear up, man. I've been in tighter corners.' But Randall didn't sound very convinced as another volley of bullets made them hit the deck and keep their heads down for dear life.

'Hey, *amigo*!' Pancho Rodriguez called out. 'You hear that? Sounds like they're hunting bear or somet'ing.'

Tex Petersen could hardly not hear the clatter of

rifle fire echoing through the hills to them from some adjoining canyon. 'Sounds more like a battle goin' on, if you're asking me. Let's go take a look.'

'No! We don' want to get involved in nuthin' like that,' the tubby Mexican shouted after his friend, as the Texan spurred his Appaloosa forward up a steep slope. 'Wait for me!'

They had climbed their broncs up through the Loveland Pass from Denver gradually reaching an elevation of 11,000 feet beneath the towering 14,000 feet Mount Lincoln. The shooting sounded to be coming from the far side of one of its spurs and Petersen was already riding around the side of a thick forest of lodgepole pines to reach the top of the tree-line.

When his grey-spotted horse bounded up on to the crest he was greeted by the awesome sight of the upper Arkansas River valley stretching before him, the stream just a silver ribbon trickling between the Mosquito range stretching southwards on the eastern side, and on the far side the Sawatch mountains. Its five 'fourteeners', as they were called, magnificent peaks, their height guessed at, but as yet to be measured or even given names, billowed away like icy white sails.

'Whoo!' Tex gave a whistle of awe. 'It's like being on top of the world.'

Pancho reined in his mustang as he joined him, more interested in the shooting than the scenery.

'There they are,' he cried, pointing to a man in a

sombrero perched on the edge of a craggy gulch. Puffs of gunsmoke revealed the presence of two other bushwhackers on the other side. 'Who they fire at?'

Tex leaped from the Appaloosa, his Winchester carbine in his hand, and climbed down the perilous descent to where the ridge was carved apart by the narrow Skinned Alive canyon. He peered over and had a bird's eye view of the mule train, a dead, bleeding animal, and what looked like the corpse of a man. The muleteers were cowering down in the rocks. Only one man, a Yankee officer by the look of his outfit, was making a fight of it as the bushwhackers smashed bullets about him from three different directions.

'This sure ain't a fair fight,' the Texan drawled, levering the first of twelve slugs into his Winchester's breech. 'I'm gonna lend them fellas down there a hand.'

'Hey, these are my countrymen you want to kill,' Pancho protested. 'I can't help you.'

'I ain't gonna kill 'em,' Petersen muttered, as he took aim at the one on their side of the gulch. He was lower down, about 200 yards away. *Pa-dang.* His bullet ricocheted off the rock beside Luna's head making him jump around with alarm. Tex levered the carbine and let him have three more in quick succession. The Mexican spun around, stared up at them and leapt like a scalded cat for the cover of some rocks. 'Just give him a fright!'

'*Sí*,' Pancho laughed. 'He was not expecting that.'

Aristide Luna's heart was pounding. 'What the devil? Where have these sons of bitches come from?' he growled. And what kind of weapon did this man have, he wondered, for he had turned his attention to his two *compadres* on the other side of the gulch, strafing them with a stream of lead. That must have been his tenth shot. How many more had he got? And now the American *capitan* down below had joined in the attack. 'Hell take them!' Luna cried.

He was at a disadvantage, especially as his own Springfield rifle was a single shot, converted from muzzle-loader to breech-loader. He fumbled in the pocket of his leather jacket for another brass-cased cartridge, but it took valuable time to insert one, re-cock, take aim and fire at their new assailant. But at least the shot whining away past this *hombre*'s Stetson made him keep his distance.

As Luna reloaded, he heard one of his *vaqueros*, Jorge, cry out shrilly and clutch at his upper arm as blood began to seep through his fingers.

'Hurrah!' Aaron Rooney shouted, brandishing his fist. 'We got one of the murthering devils.'

'Yes, but not the one I wanted, the one who killed Mr Callaghan. There he is! We've got him rattled.' Captain Randall took aim at the Mexican as he showed himself. 'Nearly!' He snapped off another shot or two as the murderer went leaping away along the ridge. 'We've got him on the run.'

'But who is that up there?' Rooney peered upwards at the stranger, attired in range clothes, who was now standing, firing from the shoulder, making the bushwhackers jump for their lives. 'Hey, sir! Look there's another greaser standing up behind him. Quick, get him.'

'No.' The captain studied the two men on the ridge. 'He's not shooting. I think they're together.'

Aristide Luna had had enough. This was not on his agenda. Where had these two come from out of the blue? Who were they? Had the mineowner hired protection? His ancient single shot was no match for their repeaters. '*Muchachos!*' he yelled, signalling to his men with his rifle. 'Come on! We're getting out.' At least, he thought, as he went leaping and dodging away along the ridge to find his teth- ered horse, he had killed the engineer.

'Let me have a shot at him, sir,' Rooney begged, poking his ruddy-nosed, pugnacious head above the rim.

Randall handed him the Spencer and Rooney hugged it into his shoulder and wildly cracked off a shot. 'Missed the bastard!'

'You're not allowing for the strong wind. Try again.'

But by the time his foreman had loosed the seventh and final bullet the bushwhackers had disappeared from sight. Up on the ridge Petersen spotted the one on their own side emerge from

some rocks astride a mustang and go wildly whipping him away down some sort of goatpath. 'He's
outa range now,' he said.

'*Sí.*' Pancho waved a friendly greeting to those in
the gulch below. 'Hey, we sure saved your bacon,
amigos. A few seconds later and you would be dead
pork.'

'Maybe I can climb down to 'em for a chat? I
wanna find out what this is all about.' Tex tossed his
carbine to the fat Mexican. 'You stay here with the
horses.'

'You no kidding. You won't catch me climbin'
down there.'

Captain Randall watched the lithe young
Westerner in his flapping cowhide chaps, buckskin
shirt, high-heeled boots and revolver slung on one
hip, starting to make the perilous descent of the
overhanging cliff. 'Stop! he shouted. 'I wouldn't do
that. It's too risky.'

But the Texan's lariat, attached to a jutting rock,
came snaking down, and he was leaping out, sliding
fast down it with his gloved hands, bouncing on his
heels from rock to rock. The rope ran out but he
made the last leap and landed lightly on the balls of
his toes beside them. 'Howdy,' he grinned, offering
his hand.

'Where on earth did you spring from?' Randall
eagerly grasped it to shake. 'If you hadn't arrived I
fear we would have been dead ducks.'

'The captain put up a fine fight,' Rooney butted

in. 'But they had us pinned down.'

'What were they after?'

'Silver ore.' Randall nodded at the panniers. 'I've got a claim higher up the creek. These scum are trying to run us off.'

'And they nearly succeeded, the murdering swine.' Rooney grabbed hold of Tex to pump his gloved hand. 'Let me thank you, mister. You saved my men's lives.'

'Alas, they have killed my engineer,' Randall said. 'Cut him down in cold blood. A fine fellow. He never hurt anyone.'

'Captain, is it?' Tex asked. 'You with the blue pants?'

'Up until last year I was. Now I'm a civilian.'

'Jeez,' Tex drawled. 'Never thought I'd be saving the skin of some damn Yankee.'

'Were you in the war?'

'No, but my daddy was. Joined Wharton's Texas Rangers' brigade. Fought at Shiloh. Came home without one leg. Still, I guess he was lucky to come home at all.'

'The war's over now. There's been too much bitterness. We've got to put it behind us.'

'Easy enough to say. There's them in the south ain't likely to fergit in a hurry their houses put to the flames by your conquering heroes, the ruination of it all.' Tex's grey eyes glinted fiercely as he met the captain's. But he shrugged and added more softly, 'I guess, as you say, it's time to start anew. That's what me and my *amigo* up there are looking to do. Any idea where we can find a free claim?'

'You want to go into the mining game?' Randall sounded surprised. 'Forgive me, but you don't look the sort to swing a pick.'

'We're lookin' to git rich an' we'll do whatever has to be done. Not that I know damn all about it, but I can learn.'

'What's your normal occupation?'

'Waal,' Tex grinned, amiably, 'we've been two months coming up the Goodnight-Loving trail with a thousand head of longhorns. Not my property, I might point out. We're just a couple of cowboys. Came up from San Angelo, through the Horsehead Crossing, fightin' off Comanch' most of the time. We got paid off at Cheyenne and made our way back to Denver. It was there we heard the talk of some fella gettin' rich as Croesus in Oro City.'

'Mr Tabor's done well for himself, but it's not so easy for us others. He's already bought up most claims which might bring success. Still, I'm not trying to dishearten you. Everybody's welcome to try. It's a free country.'

Tex nodded at the loaded mules. 'How about *your* finds?'

'Promising. But it's early days yet.' The captain's ruddy countenance darkened. 'And now it seems I've got a war on my hands trying to hang on to my claim. It's obvious these people would have no scruples about killing us all.'

'Who are they?'

'I have no idea,' Randall muttered.

But Rooney butted in. 'Lousy stinking greasers. What we need is protection, Captain. My men ain't gunslingers.' He waved an arm along at the glum-looking labourers, two Irishmen, two scruffy Anglos, and a couple of Poles. 'You're gonna have to pay them danger money or you'll have them deserting, that's for sure.'

Randall watched them attending to the one of their number who had been hit in the foot. 'You stick with me,' he said. 'We'll discuss extra payment when we get to town. We'll take Mr Callaghan in and bury him there.'

He turned back to Tex, eyed him for a few moments and burst out, 'Young fellow, you seem handy with a gun. How would you like to work for me?'

'No suh. My guns ain't for hire,' Petersen drawled. 'Killin' Comanch' is the most I've ever done. I'm a peace-loving man. No, me and my pardner will be moseying on, see what we can see. This is no fight of mine.'

'Too bad,' Randall mused, as he watched him climb up out of the gulch and grab the end of his rope, then start to haul himself back up the cliff again. 'So long, cowboy. Thanks again. The best of luck to you.'

THREE

Don Demetrio del Hasta de Luna was a man old before his time, crippled by a gunshot to his spine, embittered by the loss of his once vast lands stolen from him by the *Yanquis.* Once he had run 10,000 head of cattle on one of the renowned *ranchos* of Taos. He had been a *don* of high-standing, presiding over his *vaqueros*, manservants and maids in feudal manner. But those days were gone.

For centuries his family had taken a leading role in that far-flung outpost of the Mexican empire stretching north from Santa Fe. The war with the US had ruined all that. After their marines fought their way into Mexico City vast tracts of land had been ceded to the States: Texas, California, Arizona and his own land in New Mexico.

Shyster Yankee lawyers had closed in on him like packs of hyenas and it was decreed by their crooked courts that he no longer had title to his lands. They were sold off to *Americanos.* Since then *Don*

Demetrio had harboured a bitter hatred for the whole race.

His fortune eroded, he and his wife and family had been forced to move north into the Territory of Colorado where they settled a sparse and rocky piece of land amid the hostile environment of the higher Arkansas valley. His wife, Eva, had christened their new home Buena Vista, but that was about all that could be said for it, the magnificent views of mountain peaks on either side.

To rub salt into his wounds, not far from there his family had owned a silver mine in the canyon the Americans had re-named Skinned Alive Creek, but it was believed all its riches had long since run out. Imagine his surprise when he heard that the mine was in production again. It had been claimed by one of the hated Yankees, a Captain Randall.

Demetrio had hired an English-speaking lawyer and taken his case and his ancient deeds to the mining court of Denver on the far north-east side of the hills. He had been told that his deeds no longer held any legal significance and that Randall's claim was confirmed.

Oh, he knew he was not the only disenfranchised Mexican, or *former* Mexican, to be robbed blind by the scheming *Americanos*, but he had sworn vengeance and was determined to get back his family's mine.

Today, in his wooden wheelchair, he sat on his veranda and watched an expert horseman on a spirited mount come galloping up towards their small *rancho*. It was his oldest son, Aristide, and it looked as if he was in a hurry. Behind him loped Raoul and Jorge.

'So?' he demanded, as Aristide swung from the saddle of his sweated-up mount. 'What is your news?'

Aristide clambered up on to the veranda, his razor-sharp features sullen. He divested himself of his leather jacket and sombrero and filled a glass from a flask of wine on a table before he spoke. He stood there in his black velveteen shirt, his *chapare-jos* buckled down their sides by silver conchos, gave more a snarl than a smile and announced, 'I have killed one of the pigs for you.'

'Who?' his father demanded, eagerly. 'The *jefe*?'

'No, the fat one, Callaghan.'

'You fool, I told you to kill Randall. You cut off the head of a snake, not its tail.'

'If I do your killing for you, I decide who I kill. The engineer was the most important. Without him they cannot operate the mine.'

'Of course they can, you dolt. They hire another engineer.'

'Don't call me a dolt. It is I who is putting his life on the line. Who else is there to fight with me. You? My brother, Rafael? Your few ancient *vaqueros*? No, I am on my own.'

'You dare to speak to me like that?' The silver-haired *don*'s dark face creased with a look of agony as he struggled to reach for his bullwhip and nearly fell from his chair. 'You are not too old for a good thrashing.'

His wife hurried from the single-storey adobe *casa* to hold her husband back in his chair. 'Aristide, have you no respect? Why must you always fight your father?'

'I would not fight a cripple.' The younger Mexican swilled back more wine and spat out the words in contempt. 'But I'm not taking insults from that useless old man.'

'I might remind you I own this ranch. What gold still remains to this family is in my safe. You do as I say, you ungrateful lout, or I will disown you, cast you off without a *centavo*.'

'Huh?' Aristide spread his hands and shrugged his shoulders, looking around at the house and the land. 'You think I give a damn?'

'You *will* do when we are rich, when we own that mine again.'

'Pah! You won't own any mine unless you get us some decent weapons.' He tossed the Springfield clattering away into a corner. 'This single shot is useless. The *Americanos* have repeaters. They have a marksman working for them, too.'

The *don* sat straight-backed in his chair. 'Come on, Aristide. We must not argue. We must devise a plan. I am prepared to pay out good money to get Randall. What you must do is ride into Oro City. You must hire a couple of professional killers, too.

28

There are plenty hanging about the gambling dens. We will pay them to kill that Yankee dog. I will buy you the best rifle there is. If they hire killers so will we.'

'All right.' Aristide twisted his lips in a distasteful grimace. 'I will do that, if I can. What about paying me the same rate as those men?'

'You will get your reward when the mine is ours. We all will. Our family will be one to be proud of again.'

'Oh, you think so? Where's my precious brother?'

'Out on the range,' his mother said, going to squeeze her son's shoulder. 'Rafael does not have the same fighting spirit as you.'

'No, he's a damned milksop.'

'That's as maybe,' she consoled. 'All I want is that *gringo* Randall's head brought here. I will serve his *cojones* for you on a platter. Think, Aristide, how good it will be to be rich.'

Rafael Luna, however, was not out on the range. He was, at that moment, cracking his long bullwhip over the backs of a bunch of wild horses he had rounded up and secretly broken in a little-known box canyon some way from their range. For a youth of barely twenty years he possessed great horse mastership, as it was termed.

'Hai-yai!' he cried, as he rode into Oro City, driving the dozen broncs before him. But, as a dog suddenly rushed out, snarling and snapping, his deep-chested grey mare shied to one side. It did not faze Rafael. Instinctively, he swung the horse to skip sideways, and a stinging crack from the whip made the mongrel howl and run whining away.

Rafael headed the bunch around town to avoid the mainstreet mud and folks turned to watch the handsome young Mexican who seemed to have attained a perfect equilibrium with his mount, as if the two were one, and admire the ease with which he guided the rough and scrubby bunch along to Gomez's corral. The horse dealer saw him coming and swung open his gate so the wild ones could stream in.

'So, you haven't branded them yet?'

'No,' Rafael replied. 'I leave that up to you. If you want them.'

Gomez eyed them, craftily, through narrowed lids. And made a few derogatory remarks. 'That one's got a dipped back! That other's flat-sided!' – meaning his ribs were not well-rounded.

'What do you expect? These are half-wild horses. If you don't want them I'll soon find other buyers.'

'Is that black stallion the leader of the bunch?' Gomez went on criticizing. 'I don't like the look of him. A restless eye means a tricky disposition.'

'He's never been into a town before. It's riled him. I've ridden him. He'll soon settle down.'

'Does your father know you're selling these?'

'They're not his. I caught them along the valley, tricked them into a box canyon. The black's a fine horse. I won't part with him for less than twenty dollars. The others you can have for ten each.'

'But they all need to be shoed. Whose gonna buy these frisky brutes?'

'I, for one, like a spirited horse. Don't be too hard on them, Señor Gomez. They need to keep their spirit.'

The dealer finally settled on a price, handed it over in silver dollars and asked, 'You going into business on your own, Rafael? Your father won't like this.'

'*Sí*, I am tired of working on the range for no reward but my keep. I need to make something of myself. To tell you the truth I wish to be married.'

'Oh, yes.' Gomez shrilled a few profane remarks in Spanish. 'So, who's the lucky girl?'

Rafael gave a flashing smile from beneath the shade of his sombrero. 'That, my friend, is my business.'

He sent his mount proudly stepping away by the pressure of his knees behind the girths. The vicious rowels of his spurs were mainly for show, not use. Unlike many men in those parts Rafael loved horses and tried to be kind to them.

It was all very well saying he planned to be married. What worried him was that the young lady in question, Lucille Langridge, was not yet aware of that fact. Nor would his parents be pleased that he wished to leave their fold and take an Anglo as a wife. He well knew his father's hatred of the breed.

Nonetheless, he swung down from the grey, Maria, and hitched her to the rail outside the Langridge gun store, jumping up confidently on to the sidewalk. A bell jangled as he pushed open a glass-fronted door. '*Buenas tardes,*' he cried, for the sun was already sinking low behind the mountains, illuminating the snowy peaks in a ruddy glow.

'Good evening to you, Rafael,' Careen replied. 'How can I help you?'

'This revolver.' He produced an old Colt. 'The cylinder has come adrift. I don't know. Can you repair it?'

Careen took a look. 'I doubt it. The whole mechanism's broken. How long have you had this? It's made of cheap iron. Must be before Colt started importing Sheffield steel from England.'

'It's always been serviceable.' In fact, the revolver was mainly an excuse to call in the shop. Rafael was too shy to broach his true purpose. He tried to peer through a door into the workroom of the store. 'Is your sister here tonight?'

'Yes, she's making dinner.' Careen took his arm and showed him their range of pistols arrayed in a glass-topped case. 'You can throw that old thing away. Here, take your choice. How about this nice Smith & Wesson with the ivory grip. Only twenty-five dollars.'

'Can I go through to speak to her?'Rafael blurted out.

'Speak to her?' The older sister's lips smiled with

curious amusement. 'What do you want with Lucille?'

'I . . . I just wish to see her.'

'Do you want to make a purchase or not?'

'*Sí*, I will try that one.' He indicated the Smith & Wesson. 'Is it a self-cocker?'

'Yes. Shall I show you how to fire it? It's got a different pull to the ones you're used to.'

'Yes, if you will. Then, perhaps, I can speak to Lucille?'

Careen held the revolver in her hand across her breast and eyed him, severely. 'You seem a nice young man, Rafael. But I think I must tell you: forget Lucille. She's not for you.'

'Why not? Because I'm Mexican?'

'That may have something to do with it. But mainly because you have little to offer her. I have acted as my sister's protector since our mother died, almost a second mother to her. Yes, she is of marriageable age. But her husband must be a man of some substance. Not some . . . some. . . .'

'Greaser? Second-class citizen? You think I'm not good enough for her?'

'You said it, not me. But, yes, I have to think of her future. Pay for the gun and go, Rafael. Leave her alone. OK?'

'No, it is not OK,' the young Mexican said, his dark, languorous eyes suddenly haughty and proud as he paid for the revolver and stuffed it in the crimson sash around his slim waist. 'I will go. But I will not give up hope.'

'Here!' Careen tossed a box of cartridges to him, contemptuously, as he opened the door. 'You need these. It fires .44s. You can have them on the house.'

Rafael scowled at her and returned to slap two more dollars on to the counter. 'I pay for what I buy.'

As he left the store and leaped on to his grey, swinging her away, angrily, and setting off at a gallop out of town and back towards the hills, Lucille came out into the shop and saw him go.

'What's wrong with Rafael?' she cried. 'Didn't he ask for me?

'No,' Careen replied.' He was just buying a gun.'

FOUR

Tex Petersen was surprised to see so much activity in Oro City, folks going hither and thither, ploughing through the mud on foot, pulling pack mules, or whipping at wagon teams. The main street was littered with lumber and building materials as yet another store of some sort was erected. And every other one seemed to be a saloon, billiards parlour, or whorehouse. So he and Pancho opted for one called Rosie's, which was a mix of all three.

The place was jam-packed, the roulette wheel spinning non-stop, wagers placed with pouches of silver, weighed by a tattooed lady at the bar operating the scales. Prices were sky-high. Boom-town prices. Tex winced at the absence of change from a dollar for two tumblers of whiskey drawn from a barrel.

'That's nuthin',' an ancient, bearded panhandler sang out. 'Rosie'll charge ye a dollar fer one of them hard-biled eggs.'

'Ees that her?' Pancho asked, big eyes goggling at a large *madame*, her hair hennaed, her face rouged, a necklace coiled beneath her numerous chins, and flashing rings on her pudgy hands. Her green velveteen dress strained to contain a vast bosom as, arms akimbo she checked the activities. 'What a lovely lady. Get an eyeful of those milkjugs!'

'Yeah, she's just your type, *amigo*, but I doubt if you could afford her. At least, not 'til we've made our fortune.'

Tex had asked around to see if anybody had a claim to sell. 'Seems like everybody in the whole darn town wants to sell one and the cheapest is a hundred dollars.'

'How we know they any good?'

'We don't. That's the problem.'

The tall, lean cowhand, who stood a good head-and-shoulders above most other men in the saloon, looked around him and spotted a familiar face lounging, glass in hand, at one of the tables. 'There's that no-good crafty rattlesnake, Luke Short. Let's go jine him, Pancho ol' pal. But don't let him inveigle you into a game. He'll skin your hide.'

Short was attired in clean linen, a bootlace tie held by a silver longhorn woggle, a natty, crossover waistcoat, with a gold watch and chain, and a velvet-collared frock coat. His pants were tight nankeen and his boots highly-polished in spite of the mud outside. It was an era of famed gambling men and professional killers. Luke had not as yet achieved the notoriety of Wyatt Earp, Doc Holliday or Bat Masterson, but he had a growing reputation as a fast and deadly shot.

'Howdy,' Tex drawled, sitting on a barrel on the opposite side of the table to Short and leaning his back against the wooden wall. 'Fancy meetin' you again. Take a pew, Pancho.'

Short was average height, about five seven, a handsome enough young man, but his black hair slicked back with brilliantine from his face of barroom pallor, and dark eyes flickering through eye-slits gave him a snake look. His face was clean shaven, apart from a pencil moustache, revealing a weak chin.

'Do I know you gents?' he countered.

'Sure, we're fellow Texans. I sat in a game with you down in San Antone. And I saw you in Dodge.'

Luke glanced at Pancho witheringly. 'I wasn't aware Mexicans could be called Texans.'

'Oh, *sí*,' Pancho exclaimed. 'We are part of your empire. Me, I born in Meh-ico. But it part of Texas now. So, I'm a Texican.'

Short turned away, disregarding them, leaning his back against the wall too, and flipping out a pack of cards to catch them with great adroitness.

Petersen shrugged, winked at Pancho, took a sup of his whiskey, and a look at a much-thumbed newspaper, the *Kansas City Times*, which was lying on the table. 'Waal, whadda ya know,' he drawled eventually. 'Some fella named Bell's bin demonstratin' a talkin' machine. Calls it the telephone. But President Hayes says he can't understand what possible use it will ever be, or why anybody should want one.'

'Thass crazy, man. The president must be brainy to be in the White House,' Pancho put in, 'but even I can see a use for a talking wire. A rancher could have one to order his groceries. Save him having to come into town. Or the Indians could declare war on it!'

'Why don't you write to the president and tell him?' Luke Short snapped. 'Don't tell me, 'cause, buddy, I ain't interested.'

'In that case you must have much in common with the president. Both men of blinkered vision,' Tex remarked. 'So, you got outa Dodge, eh, Luke, 'fore they run you out?'

'What are you talking about?' Short turned on him, snarling, 'Why don't you coupla sage rats go bother somebody else? Or, better still, go visit the bath-house. You ain't the kinda company I care to keep.'

'No need to be nasty, Luke,' Tex protested. 'Just heard on the grapevine that you got accused of cheatin' in the Longbranch at Dodge. Nearly come to gunplay, didn't it?'

'Yep. And if you don't shut your mouth it might come to that again, mister. Who invited you smelly varmints to sit here and talk to me?' Luke's face flushed to his temples. 'In other words, get lost.'

'Waal, good for you in ignoring whoever it was called you a cheat,' Petersen drawled, unflummoxed. 'You showed admirable restraint. Otherwise one of you might have ended up dead. You did the right thing in gettin' outa town and lettin' the situation cool down.'

'It wouldn't have been me dead, it would have been that loudmouth fool. No question about that.'

'No, the question is, did you or didn't you?'

'What?'

'Deal from the bottom of the pack.'

'I don't need to,' Luke said. 'Why, you fancy a game?'

'Aw, no,' the cowboy replied. 'Picture cards ain't my strong suit. Geddit?'

'Nor's washing, neither, apparently.'

Tex grinned as Short wrinkled his nose and flicked dust from his frock coat, fastidiously. 'Point taken. That rings a bell, as Mr Bell might say. Ain't had a bath in a month or more. Say, Pancho, how about you and me go visit the Chinese Celestial Bath House, then eat someplace? I've a feelin' we ain't welcome here. See ya around, Luke.'

'I hope not,' the gambler muttered and, as he watched the tall one and the short fat one push their way out through the throng, muttered to himself, 'Were those two jokers trying to rile me?'

If so, they had succeeded. Luke felt very edgy. *What* were they talking about? Professional

39

gamblers used every ruse in the book, from a marked deck to an ace up the sleeve. The trick was not to get spotted. He had slipped up in Dodge, but it wouldn't happen again. The sheriff, Bat Masterson, had advised him to get out of town. When Bat offered such advice it wasn't wise to ignore him. So Luke had taken the next train on the new railroad out across the plains to Pueblo. He would have preferred to go on to Santa Fe, but the railroad boys had stopped in their tracks, yet to come to an agreement with the old frontiersman, Dick Wootton, who claimed to own the toll trail across Raton Pass. So Luke had taken the stage-coach up to Oro City, instead. He had not expected word of his little contretemps at Dodge to have spread so soon. It would not ensure him a welcome in the casinos. Maybe that tall blabbermouth Texan found it amusing. Luke felt for the pearl-handled revolver shoulder-hung beneath his coat, anger seething in him. 'Maybe I need to shut his mouth.'

Captain Randall left his hotel the next morning and climbed up the hill to the new smelting works set up by Horace Tabor. 'I got good news for you,' Tabor beamed from behind his enormous moustache. 'That carbonate of lead you brought in contains two pounds of silver to the ton. That's almost as much as mine.'

'Good Lord!' For moments Randall was dumb-struck, 'What would you suggest I do now?'

'I could handle the transaction for you.' By now Horace had graduated from one diamond ring to another sparkling stone on his other hand and cufflinks to match. He had togged himself out in a loud check suit and silver-knobbed cane. 'I'm sending a load of silver down to Denver under Wells Fargo armed guard. They'll give me a good price and ship it on by railroad to New York. I could take yours. Of course I'd need my cut.'

Randall eyed the cocky little fellow who had started life as a poor Vermont stonecutter and prospered largely due to his wife's steely astuteness and industry. 'Perhaps I'll deal with them on my own. I see they've opened an office up here.'

'You're entitled to do that,' Horace replied, somewhat aggrieved. 'I should warn you not many small mines make the grade. You have to think big in this game. Of course, you've no idea how deep your vein goes. It could peter out in a couple of weeks. Then you say you've got all this bother with bandits targeting you. I'd be willing to take a gamble and buy you out. How's $10,000 sound?'

'It sounds a lot, my friend, but it also makes me suspect the Skinned Alive might be worth treble that.'

'Tell you what, I'm feeling in a magnaminous mood this fine morning! Why don't we take a buggy ride out to the Matchless? I'll show you the ropes, Captain.'

He might have preferred to lord it in The Golden

Garter casino, but once he struck rich Tabor had been quick not only to protect his interests but capitalize on them.

When they reached his deep shaft, the captain saw he had it fenced off by high barbed wire strung between posts. He had recruited armed guards, had iron doors and shutters padlocked across any building of importance and was in the process of constructing a cage to be lowered 200 feet vertically into the ground. It was the scene of much industry. 'Me and my two partners are getting twenty thousand dollars a week outa here,' he boasted.

He invited Randall into his office and offered him the best French brandy from a cut-glass decanter, but the captain demurred, saying he liked to keep a clear head at this time of day.

Horace indicated a huge iron safe with a newfangled pin tumbler cylinder safety lock provided by Linus Yale, Jnr. 'No cracksman would get in this,' he said as he produced a flat key and swung open the door. He took wads of notes and offered them to Randall. 'There y'are, Captain. I'll up my offer to fifteen thousand. You can have it now. All I need's your handshake and signature to the transfer.'

'No, thanks, Tabor, old chap. It's not the money I'm particularly interested in. I could retire comfortably enough back East on my army pension. But I love the great outdoors and the excitement of mining appeals to me.'

'Aw, well, I'll have to wait 'til you git shot by one

of them greasers who's runnin' you off,' Horace
said, huffily. 'Then I'll git it a lot cheaper.'

'They're not going to run me off.'

'I wouldn't be so sure about that, Captain.
They've already got your engineer. How are you
gonna mine it now?'

'I'm learning fast,' Randall replied. 'I'd better be
getting back to town. I've got a lot to do today.'

'Me, too,' Horace exclaimed, slamming the safe
shut and thrusting one of the wads of notes in his
pocket. 'I'm due in a poker game. You want to join
us?'

'No, I'm not a gambling man. Thanks all the
same. I want to try to find two or three reliable
bodyguards like yours.'

'Ah, I fear you'll have bad luck. I've snapped up
the best of 'em for my other mines. All that's left is
the usual drunken riff-raff.'

'You've got other mines?'

'Sure have. I ain't been wasting my time, much as
Augusta might think so. I've bought up a dozen
others, let's see' – he began counting on his fingers
– 'the Little Pittsburgh, the Chrysolite, the Scooper,
Union Emma, Tam O'Shanter, the Henrietta, the
Hibernia, May Queen, Elk and Wheel of Fortune,
and what's the other, oh, I forget. I got so much
cash coming in I dunno what to do with it all. Did
you hear of my plan to build a big opera house?'

'Yes, vaguely.'

'I'm having real bricks shipped in from the East.

None of your timber construction. The opry house-'ll be my lasting monument.'

'Really?' As Tabor sent the buggy wheeling back towards town Randall reflected on how sudden wealth sent some men demented. Maybe it would have been best to take Horace's offer. Maybe the Skinned Alive would not yield much at all. He just didn't like being pushed. Never had. Not by Apaches. Not by crooked traders. Not by Mexicans. Not by jumped-up millionaires. 'A simple cross on my grave'll do me as a monument,' he said.

'Don't speak too soon!' Tabor chortled all the way back to town at his joke. Who did this toffee-nosed army captain think he was? He's a nobody, he thought, compared to me.

FIVE

Coal Oil Johnny, as they called him, had tumbled into the gunshop with cans of kerosene for their lanterns. 'That's three seventy-five a gallon, miss,' he sang out to Lucille who was about to pay him from the till.

'What?' Careen exploded. 'Are you crazy? Nobody's going to pay nearly four dollars for a can of oil.'

'You're wrong there, ma'am. It's gawn up in view of the fluctuating market. Everything's gawn up. I'm forced to keep my prices in line to make a living in this town. It ain't my fault. That's the way it is. Iffen you don't want it, there's plenty that does.' Johnny picked up the can as if to take it away again.

'Leave it,' Careen shrilled. 'Pay him, Lucille.'

'Thanks. Way thangs are going it may well be four dollars next week.'

'It's terrible,' Lucille remarked as they watched him go out to his cart. 'Since all these people arrived everything's gone up and up and up sky-high.'

'There's only one answer. We'll have to put up our prices, too,' Careen said. 'I guess it's the law of supply and demand. What do *these* characters want, I wonder?'

She was eyeing two weatherbeaten *hombres* who were pushing into the shop, a tall one badly in need of a shave, and a fat Mexican smirking at them from beneath a droopy moustache.

'How can I help you?' she snapped.

'Need some ammo, ma'am.' Tex stroked his jaw as he appraised the fine-looking redhead with her flashing green eyes and wished they'd visited the barber shop before it closed the previous night. He was quite taken by her. 'Run outa .44s for my Winchester.'

'Nice weapon,' Careen replied. 'May I take a look?'

'Sure, it's the latest model, the '73.' Petersen handed the carbine across. 'Twelve cartridge mag.'

'I know what it is.' Careen deftly levered it to check it was empty. 'Give me some centre fire .44s, Lucille.'

When the girl passed a box of a dozen to her she nimbly inserted them into the tubular magazine beneath the barrel. She levered a fresh slug into the chamber, held the carbine across her chest, ready-cocked. 'Would you care to follow me into the back yard?'

'Lead on.' Pancho swept off his sombrero and bowed deeply. 'An invitation by so beautiful a lady is our command.'

Careen, stern-faced, ignoring the flattery, led the way out. At one end of the fenced yard, where hens were pecking, were hanging two rag dummies. She took a stance and carefully fired a volley. The bullets ploughed into the chest of one of the dummies, making the chickens squawk and scurry for cover. 'Bull's-eye.' She flicked back the lid covering the top of the iron frame.

'You sure know how to handle it,' Tex remarked, with a whistle of approval.

'It's my job. I've been firing rifles since I was eight and I wouldn't like to tell you how long ago that was.' She weighed the carbine in her hand. 'Nice balance. We don't see many of these in here.'

'Stronger, simpler, lighter. That sliding lid keeps out the rain and snow from the mechanism too.'

'Yes, a good idea.'

Tex believed in striking while the iron was hot, so to speak. 'How about stepping out with me tonight, lady? I figure we could have an interesting conversation. And, what's more, you're the tastiest-looker I seen since I left Texas.'

'And you, my friend, have all the allure of some charbroiled vagrant.' She tossed the carbine back at him hard. 'Pay for your slugs and clear out.'

Petersen held her gaze for a few seconds, smiled slightly and drawled, 'Cain't blame a man for tryin'.

Come on, Pancho, it sure is time to take that bath.'

'The nerve of the man!' Careen watched them go. 'He only tried to proposition me out in the yard.'

Lucille smiled, brightly. 'Tall, dark and handsome. What more could you want? I thought he was rather nice.'

'Huh!' For some reason Careen's heart was pounding hard. It was not often a man had this effect on her. There was something about the stranger's intense regard, his lazy smile, as if he could read her mind. 'I've met too many of his kind. They're dangerous, Lucille. Be warned. They bring a girl only heartache. What you need, and I need, is a solid, steady man.'

As if in answer to her prayer Captain Randall suddenly stepped through the door. 'Why, hello.' Careen's face lit up in a smile, for he was one of the few 'cultivated' men in this town. 'We were so sorry to hear of Mr Callaghan. Why should anyone want to murder him?'

'That's what I'd like to know,' Randall replied, gruffly. 'By his appearance the assassin and his friends were Mexicans. But that's all I know.'

'Poor Mr Callaghan,' Lucille sympathized. 'Such a jolly man. What a shock. I was only talking to him a couple of weeks ago.'

'Trouble and killing. It seems to follow us every-where.' Their father, gaunt-faced, with a shock of white hair, had come from the workshop. He was

48

wearing a leather apron, a hammer and punch still in his hands. 'This town's gone to the devil. There's no law and order any more. Is there no chance of catching the miscreant?'

'Well, Mr Langridge, you know what it's like in Oro. Everybody's too busy scratching for silver to worry about men getting killed. We've no police force and the nearest army outpost's two hundred miles away.'

'Dreadful.' Langridge had sunk into a deep melancholy since his son, Stephen, had been killed in the war, hanged by the Federals as a spy. Nothing but trouble. Careen's three-year-old daughter, a sickly child, dead of the fever. The trouble *she* had gotten into. His own wife dying giving birth to Lucille. The war had ended ten years ago but the old man had never seemed to get over his shock and sorrow.

Added to that was the need to get away from his beloved homeland, Tennessee, cross the Mississippi and head west, get as far away as he could to some-place where they would be unknown, for his life was in danger and that of Careen, too.

'The burial's tomorrow,' Randall announced, 'if you'd care to attend.'

'Of course we will,' Careen put in and, trying to look on a brighter side, asked, 'How are *you*, Captain? How is the mine?'

She hoped her question did not betray a note of self-interest for, to tell the truth, she had heard a rumour that Randall had struck a rich vein. He might be a good deal older than her and, so far, had aroused no great spark of passion in her breast but, as her father had more than once indicated, Randall was a fine gentleman and a very marriageable prospect. Even more so if he had struck it rich.

'Please call me Robbie.' The captain's eyes twinkled. 'I think I can confide in you that the mine is doing very nicely as some person unknown has already discovered. That's the reason for my call. I intend to arm my labourers. I'd like half-a-dozen of the best carbines you have available.'

'I'm afraid I've only got a couple of the Spencer seven-shots like yours,' Langridge told him, going to the gun-rack. 'Everybody's arming themselves. We've never been so busy. I've got more on order but they haven't come through. You'll be the first to know when they arrive. We've plenty of revolvers or shotguns, take your pick.'

'Well, my men are no Dead Eye Dicks. All we need is something to scare them off. But I certainly don't plan to let these people take my mine.'

'Well said,' Careen replied, 'only—'

'Don't fret, they're not going to put me in my box just yet. And, before we get down to business, I'd better out with it. How about joining me for dinner tonight, Miss Langridge?'

'Careen,' she corrected. 'I'd be honoured.'

'There's not much choice, but that Italian,

50

Guiseppe's, seems to be a more salubrious establishment.'

'I'll be ready at eight,' she said later, after Randall had bought the two Spencers, a shotgun and revolvers for his men. 'I'll look forward to it, Robbie.'

'Good for you, Daughter,' her father commented as they went back into the workshop to join their old friend and foreman gunsmith, John Pearce. 'Don't you think so, John? It's time Careen found herself a wealthy and reliable man. She's not getting any younger.'

His daughter jagged her full lips back in a grimace. 'It's impossible. You know yourself,' she hissed, 'I'm still married.'

'So, get unmarried,' Pearce suggested.

'You both know that's not advisable,' she replied in a lowered voice, in case one of their two apprentices was listening. 'If I get in touch with his attorneys it would lead them to us.'

And, it occurred to her, as she put the coffee pot on the stove, Captain Randall might not be so enamoured of her if he knew her true history.

A furious argument was going on on the veranda of the Buena Vista ranch house as the family sat around the table after the midday lunch.

'Are you loco?' Rafael shouted at his older brother, Aristide. 'How can you be so proud of killing Callaghan? This will set all the *Americanos* against us.'

'Pah, you coward! Why do you kow-tow to them?' Aristide sneered. 'They treat us worse than blacks, worse than their dogs. To them we're lower than Indians. They think they own the world. Have you no pride?'

Their father, Demetrio, put in gruffly, as he sat in his wheelchair at head of the table, 'We are fighting for what is rightly ours. What's the matter with you, Rafael? Where's your spirit? Why won't you help us?'

'You're all fools. Can't you see the world has changed? We have to abide by the *Americanos'* laws now,' Rafael pleaded. 'Are you all crazy? You won't be happy until we are all dead.'

'I told you he was yellow,' Aristide jeered. 'All he does is skulk about out on the range. What does he do all day?'

'Boys,' their mother, Eva, commanded, 'you've got to respect each other's views. I, too, want this thieving dog, Randall, dead, but like Rafael says, you have to be cautious. We must use stealth.'

'I didn't say that at all, Mother,' Rafael protested, exasperation in his tone. 'You just don't understand. You're all living in the past.'

'Where did you suddenly get that fine gun from?' His father pointed at the Smith & Wesson stuck in Rafael's sash. 'Been robbing the stage?'

'No, it's us he's been robbing,' Aristide cried. 'He was seen selling horses to Gomez. That's where he's got his cash from.'

'What,' Señor Luna roared, reaching for his bull-whip. 'Is this true, boy?'

Rafael stood to face him in case he decided to lash out. He had had painful experience of his father's fiery temper. 'They were my horses. I caught them, broke them. They weren't on your land. I've had enough of being bullied by you. I'm going into business by myself.'

'You what?' Luna growled. 'You miserable whelp.'

'He's been sniffing around the skirts of the gunmaker's daughter,' Aristide laughed. 'He thinks if he makes himself look big in their eyes they'll let him have her. You're deluded, Rafael. You think they want anything to do with a down-at-heel greaser like you? They won't let you near.'

'I believe she loves me and I intend to take her as my bride, whether *they* like it or *you* like it,' Rafael blurted out, backing away as his father cracked the bullwhip snaking at him.

Rafael dodged the whip as his mother screamed, 'Don't, Demetrio! No, leave him.'

'You marry an Anglo bitch you disgrace us,' the old man roared. 'You will never be a son of ours again. You do as I say or get out of here.'

He cracked the lead-tipped rawhide whip again, but Rafael was ready and snatched it in his hands, jerking it to him, making his crippled father tumble, howling in wrathful agony, from his chair.

Aristide leaped up to grapple with his brother. He was six years older and had always bossed him.

But Rafael was supple. Aristide caught Rafael by his arms and twisted him over, tossing him from the veranda into the dust. Then he leaped on top of him as their mother went to the aid of her husband.

Rafael countered Aristide's leap with his boots, hurling him on his way over him. He jumped to his feet and swung a haymaker at Aristide, cracking his jaw, following up with a vicious jab into his kidneys. They began swapping blows, panting with the effort, swinging blindly. Neither would be the first to give in.

'Stop them,' Eva called, beckoning to the *vaqueros*, Raoul and Ernesto. 'They will kill each other.'

The two men, aided by other laughing ranch-hands, ran across and pulled the brothers apart, dunking their heads in the water trough and holding them under.

Aristide came up, spitting blood and water. 'Where is he?' he yelled, like a fighting cock eager to be back in the fray. So they dunked him again.

'OK, boys,' Rafael gasped. 'I've had enough.'

Raoul grinned and plonked his sombrero back on Rafael's head, letting him get to his feet. But the young Mexican wasn't amused. 'I'm going,' he shouted, looking across at his parents. 'I've had enough of you. Forget that crazy mine. Go buy another claim.' He walked across to his grey, Maria, and swung into the saddle, cantering away. 'I won't be back,' he shouted, and put her to a gallop towards Oro City.

Later when Aristide had cooled down he told the old man. 'Don't you worry, I'll settle with Randall. Give me some gold. I'll go do as you say. Buy guns, buy men. That mine will be ours again.'

Jorge had been winged in the upper arm in the last battle and did not seem too keen on another. But it was only a flesh wound. 'There's nothing wrong with you,' the older ranch foreman, Raoul, barked out. 'Come on, we ride with him.'

They leaped on their mustangs and charged away in a cloud of dust. 'I'll settle with that brother of mine, too,' Aristide hissed out. 'If I have to.'

SIX

In the days before the war life had seemed like one long sparkling summer dream. Careen's father had a prosperous gunmaking business, a large town house in Memphis with magnolia bushes and tended lawns. There were slaves and body servants, coach drives and torchlight parties. She had her own pony, attended a young ladies' academy at Lafayette, taught to dance, sing, play the piano, converse in French, to read poetry, embroider, and all the intricacies of fashion and fine behaviour. When she was still only thirteen Guy Lassiter had swept her off her feet at a summer ball. Two months later they were wed and honeymooning in New Orleans. But when they boarded the paddle steamer for home she began to notice he had a hard and callous side. She would be left in her cabin while he would be out until dawn gambling in the casino. Or so he said. She could not help notice the rouged and comely belle he spoke to in the restaurant later in the day. He was, she realized, a rake, roué, addicted gambler, a haughty and arrogant southern gentleman.

They had returned to find Memphis gone mad. Tennessee had pledged itself to fight for the Confederacy. At their welcome home party that evening General Forrest, himself, had been there. He was calling for volunteers to invade Kentucky. Guy was one of the first to rally to his flag. Soon Forrest's Raiders would be renowned and feared for their depredations in those border states. It was some of the most bitter fighting in the war, brother pitched against brother.

Careen sat before her bedroom mirror and pinned an emerald necklace around her throat, her mother's necklace, the only valuable item left of all her jewellery. The rest had been pawned to stave off starvation. She brushed back her rich auburn hair and twisted it into a topknot to pin on top with a worthless comb of paste pearls. Pretty enough, though. She wondered whether to apply a touch of a rouge to her own pale cheeks. No, better to look plain and severe. She didn't want to give Captain Randall ideas. So she chose her black silk dress, modestly buttoned to the throat and held by a cameo.

It had been OK for Guy. He had had a gay old time, galloping about, killing, looting and, no doubt, womanizing. She had been left on his estate in Tennessee with a sickly baby, Letitia, to look after, with uppity slaves and no idea how to discipline them. The estate had gone to ruin, the blood stock horses run off, before the invading Union Army reached them. She had found herself in the middle of a battlefield, the house reduced to rubble by cannon fire and, eventually, practically in rags, the baby in her arms, walked the dusty roads with other refugees, trying to get back to her father's house in Memphis.

She shuddered at the memory of a defining moment in her life. It was growing dark on a lonesome trail through a wood, her black maid, Cindy, by her side, when two Union deserters had come from the trees. It was obvious what they wanted, to rob and rape them. One, with a musket pointed at them, had a wild look. Careen had acted on impulse: she drew her revolver from the baby's shawl, shot him in the heart from point-blank range. The other man had run back into the trees screaming like a banshee. They had hurried on their way.

When she crept back into their darkened, deserted mansion in Memphis she found her father and aunt sitting like ghosts in the guttering candlelight. Their news was devastating. Her fifteen-year-old brother, Stephen, had run away and been caught trying to cross Union lines at Shiloh to reach Forrest's men. In his pocket was a scrawled map of federal defences he had sketched from a nearby hill. He had been hanged from a footbridge over

Owl Creek as that infamous battle, in which 40,000 men died, began to rage.

It had been hard for everybody in those war years, rich or poor. By scrimping and stealing they had managed to survive under Union military rule in Memphis. Her father had been ordered to reopen his gunshop to repair and manufacture arms for the Federals. What could he do? It was that or be put up against a wall and shot. But by such 'collaboration' he would be branded a traitor.

Then came the day when the comrade of the dead soldier recognized her in the street, pointed a finger, screaming, 'Murderess!' She was thrown into the garrison prison, told that Cindy had confirmed her guilt, no doubt under duress, and although she claimed self-defence, was informed by the prison commander, a tall, robust, bald-headed northerner, James McQuorkindale, that under martial law she would be hanged. Unless. . . .

Oh, yes, she knew what that 'unless' meant. Be nice to him. Very nice. At least he might have been discreet. But no, he insisted on buying her silk dresses, have her drive with him in his open landau. Soon she was his mistress, a scarlet woman, one who would be reviled when the peace came. But worse was yet in store. Much worse.

There was the sound of voices in the shop. Time to meet Captain Randall. How could she ever tell him about those events? About Guy? About McQuorkindale? About Seth, the young Union lieutenant, their brief idyll of love? About how she had tried to drive a cargo of guns to Forrest's guerillas with disastrous results. A traitor, a whore, a murderess. That's what the returning Confederates would have called her. If she had stayed in Memphis she would not only have been tarred and feathered by the populace, but hanged from the nearest telegraph pole by the Klan.

Careen took a last look in the mirror and put on her brightest smile. 'Hello, Robbie,' she called. 'I'm starving. I hope Guiseppe is on top form.'

Captain Randall was most attentive, taking her arm as they made their way along the sidewalk, seating her at the table in the candlelit dive. 'You look very beautiful tonight,' he said. 'This is a great honour to me.'

'Please don't flatter me, Robbie.'

'It's not flattery, Careen.' He placed a strong, suntanned hand over hers. 'When this trouble I'm having is over, there is something serious on my mind I wish to say to you.'

Luke Short was more than peeved. The gambler was getting the cold shoulder in the Oro City saloons. Whenever he tried to sit in on a poker game men would get up and move to another table or, worse, ignore him. His reputation was lower than a snake's belly and he blamed the tall cowboy, Petersen, for that.

He was mistaken about it. Tex hadn't mentioned

Dodge to another soul. However, it was strange how mouth-to-mouth gossip travelled on the grapevine and talk of his cheating tricks had preceded him.

Luke had only managed to sweet-talk a couple of miners into being rooked by him and they were soon out of dust. He was standing at the bar in Rosie's place when three Mexicans in range clothes ambled in, spurs jingling.

'Howdy, boys,' he said. 'You looking for action?'

'Are you Señor Short?' Aristide asked.

'Why?' Luke warily countered.

'Because we have been asking around town and your name cropped up as a man who might have his gun for hire?'

'Jine me.' Luke picked up his bottle of whiskey and found a table, filling tumblers for them with the high voltage brew. 'It's true I'm purty nifty with a six-shooter.' He patted the one beneath his frock coat. 'What are you looking for?'

Aristide's hawkish face eyed him, alertly. 'We need a man killed.' He lowered his voice and outlined their grudge against Randall. 'We don't wan' to start a backlash against us greasers. We need an Anglo, an independent gunman.'

'Sounds easy enough. What's the price on his head?'

'Two hundred dollars,' Aristide hissed. 'In gold.'

The lightly built Short made a doubtful grimace, lit a cheroot and considered the offer. Well, he wasn't making any money at cards so maybe he

61

should practise his alternative profession. 'Murder ain't to be undertaken lightly, even out here in the wilds. My price is five hundred.'

'You joke, *señor*. Three hundred. That is our highest offer. For that you run Randall and his men out of town.'

'His men? What kinda men?'

'Ach,' Raoul snarled, 'just a bunch of useless labourers.'

'What about that stranger?' Jorge put in, soothing his bandaged arm. 'He's a crack shot.'

'What stranger!' Luke asked, edgily.

'Ah, just some tall Texan who intervened. He ain't really with Randall,' Aristide remarked. 'At least, I don't think so.'

'Has he got a fat Mexican sidekick?'

'That's him. OK, I put my cards on the table. He's fast, uses one of those new Winchester repeaters. Four hundred dollars if you can take him out and Randall. We, of course, will be behind you. One hundred down and three hundred on completion.'

'Should be easy enough.' Short had no aversion to back-shooting a man in some lonely gulch. 'What nobody sees, nobody knows about. OK, boys, I'm your man. Pass the hundred across. That bastard Petersen's been asking for it.'

While these negotiations were going on Rafael was sitting on his grey mare in the darkness watching the gunshop. He had seen Careen and Randall leave, all togged up as if out for a spree. The lanterns were dowsed about nine o'clock in cabins built at the back of the store occupied by Mr Langridge, his mechanic, John, and his ancient spinster sister, Rebecca. But a light was still burning in the kitchen and the cabin occupied by one of the two sisters.

Rafael began to sing a high-pitched Mexican love lament, crooning to the moon like some crazy wolf. There was no response so he rode closer and tapped on the lighted window. The curtain was drawn back and Lucille's startled face appeared. But she smiled when she recognized the youthful Mexican.

'*Mi amor*,' he called. 'You want to come for a ride with me?'

Lucille put her fingers to her lips to quieten him, reached for her shawl and slipped out of the cabin. 'What do you want?'

'I just wan' to see you.' He flashed a smile. 'Why waste such a fine moonlit night?'

'I don't know.' She hesitated. 'Father will have a fit if he finds out. So will Careen.'

'Why worry about them?' He swung the feisty mare around, reached down, caught Lucille around her slim waist and swung her up behind him. 'Hold tight, my sweet. The tighter the better. I do not want to lose you. Right, huphup, Maria. *Arriba!*'

Sitting side-saddle across the mare's strong haunches, the girl squealed as the horse surged

63

forward up the hillside and she hung tight to Rafael. A whirl of excitement and guilt thrummed up through her as they reached a rocky path and he cantered the mare along it into the dark pine trees. How good it was to be out in the night, to feel the breeze in her hair, to hug herself close into him.

'I can't stay long,' she protested, as Raphael reached a grassy glade by a stream and reined in. He swung a boot forward over the saddle, jumped down and reached for her. 'Promise me you won't—'

'All I want is to be with you for a little while.' Rafael pulled her close into him and gently kissed her. 'Don' worry. I don' wan' to hurt you.'

He lay his Indian blanket down on the grass, produced a bottle of wine from his saddle-bag as the mare munched at the pasture. 'I have had an argument with my family. From now on I am a free man. Come, sit beside me, I will tell you—'

'I don't know. I don't want to do anything I might regret. I've never drunk wine before.' But she half lay down besides him, took a swallow of the wine. 'Mm, it's nice and sweet.' Her cheeks dimpled as she gazed at him. 'What would Aunt Becky say if she knew. Or Careen, come to that?'

Just before midnight Captain Randall escorted Careen back to the gunstore, drawing her tighter, an arm circling her waist. 'It's been a lovely evening,' he remarked. 'But I think until this trouble's blown over I'd better not be seen with you. You understand why?'

'Yes, but surely you don't think—'

'Wait,' he said, pressing her back against a shopfront and unbuttoning the holster on his belt, half-drawing and cocking the revolver. 'There's three Mexicans over there watching us.'

Careen's heart pounded as she peered across his shoulder and saw the dark silhouettes of three men in sombreros, and another man standing on a corner of the opposite sidewalk.

'There he is,' Aristide hissed. 'That's him. Now's our chance to get him.'

'Not with the woman there,' Luke Short muttered. 'Don't be such a damn fool. Anyway, I've had an idea. What's the point of killing him straight away? What you want to do is put pressure on him to sign the mine deeds over to you. If that's his lady love maybe she's the one we should concentrate on.'

'You mean kidnap her?'

'You got it, buster. Search out a derelict mine someplace near where we can hold her. Come and see me tomorrow. You need to tread carefully, use your brains in an operation like this. I'll git your mine back for ya, you'll see.'

Captain Randall protected Careen with his body, his revolver fully drawn now, and cocked in readiness as he watched the three Mexicans across the street. They were talking to an *hombre* attired like a gambler. Suddenly they unhitched mustangs, leapt in the saddles and set off at a fast pace out of town. 'Whoo,' he breathed out. 'I'm getting jittery.'

'They're probably quite harmless,' Careen laughed. 'You can't go taking potshots at every sombrero you see.'

He walked her on to the shop and as she searched for her key, he gripped her closer, stooped to kiss her lips. Careen turned her face away so the kiss brushed her cheek.

'I don't think we should, Robbie.'

'Why? Am I too old for you?'

'No, you're a fine-looking gentleman in the prime of life. I'm very honoured you find me attractive. But, no, a woman alone has to be careful. One familiarity can lead to another.'

Careen nodded across the road at a destitute girl in a shawl with a baby cradled in her arms who was begging alms from the drunken miners who spilled from the saloons. 'I wouldn't want to end up like her. I've had enough of poverty.'

'You wouldn't!' Randall looked quite shocked. 'I assure you, Careen, my intentions towards you are entirely honourable.'

'Hm,' she smiled. 'Where have I heard that before?' She unlocked and slipped inside the gunshop. 'Goodnight, Robbie. Thank you for a lovely evening. I hope it won't be too long before I see you again.'

He nodded, serious-faced, turned and walked

away as she closed the door and made her way through the darkened store. She stepped outside to the cabins at the rear of the premises. There was no light showing in Lucille's. 'I won't wake her,' Careen whispered. 'She's probably fast asleep by now.'

SEVEN

'Such wickedness!' The spindly Augusta Tabor waggled a finger and adjusted her pince-nez as she addressed a town meeting. 'Our once-peaceful town of three hundred honest souls has become a veritable Sodom and Gomorrah! A city of sin.'

Horace Tabor, with his bald dome and drooping moustache, sat uncomfortably beside her on the platform, an empty wagon at one end of the blacksmith's barn. He had been prodded into holding the meeting by his wife's scolding. 'It ain't that bad,' he groaned.

'What?' Augusta screeched. 'I have had a count made and we currently have a population of twenty thousand miners and assorted traders, not to mention females of dubious professions.'

'You mean whores?' A panhandler with a long grey beard cackled. 'Gawd bless 'em!'

'I do, indeed.' Augusta pressed on, grim-faced. 'We have counted sixty-three saloons and gaming hells, timber and tented, and no less than thirty-five brothels. It is a disgrace.'

'That's all very well, Mrs Tabor,' said Caleb Jones, a dentist and drug-store owner, 'but there's no way we can close them down. I thought this meeting was called to take action over the dreadful stench from the open sewers, the stink of dead mules left to rot in the street, and the piles of garbage everywhere.'

'That's what it is called for.' Horace Tabor had been elected town mayor. He had visions of one day being governor of Colorado so he needed to be seen to be doing good works. 'I have drawn up a plan for a system of covered sewers to drain into the Arkansas River clear of the town.'

'Thank goodness for that,' Florence Williams, a boarding-house keeper, sang out. 'Otherwise we will all be going down with typhoid.'

'Who's gonna pay for it,' Gomez, the horse dealer, asked. 'You, Horace?'

'Well, I would, but I don't see why I should.' Tabor might be a rich man but he was still canny with his cash. 'There are plenty of idle men about, those who have lost everything, been robbed, or failed to strike lucky. They can be recruited to clean up the streets at no cost to the honest citizens.'

'How do you propose to do that?' James Langridge asked.

'My good wife has pointed out that there are thirty-five bordellos operating night and day. Those women ought to pay for polluting our town with their evil behaviour. They are not short of a dollar or two.'

'They certainly ain't,' Augusta cried. 'Why that hussy who calls herself Red Stockings has a hundred thousand dollars in her bank account, all made since she arrived in our town. She started saving in my post office but then boasted she was making so much she'd have to bank with Wells Fargo.'

Tex Petersen, who had called in to see what the hullabaloo was about, gave a whistle of awe. 'Whoo! What a pity we ain't of the female gender, Pancho.'

'Maybe I could buy me a dress and go into business,' the Mexican grinned.

'Gentlemen,' Horace shouted. 'This is not a joking matter. All in favour of imposing a twenty-five dollar tax on every prostitute raise their hand.'

'Sure, why not,' Gomez said, 'if it ain't gonna cost us nuthin'. They can afford it.'

'Carried unanimously.' Horace looked at his gold watch as big as an onion. He was in a hurry to go meet a young lady of loose morals who had recently arrived in town, known as Baby Doe. 'Any other business?'

'Not so fast! Where do you think you're off to?' his wife snapped. 'Us Christian folk think it's high time we built an episcopal chapel in the town.'

'Men ain't got time to go to church,' the blacksmith, Jed Simms, said. 'They're too busy scraping for silver in all the gulches around here.'

'Yes, it's disgraceful the way observance of the

Lord's Day is ignored,' Augusta screeched. 'Drunkenness and gambling—'

'Can't you put a sack over her head, Horace?' Jed roared. 'I've heard enough. I got work to do.'

'We need a chapel, and a meeting house where folks can improve their minds?' Augusta pressed on. 'I propose we call it the Belle Esprit Society.'

'Yes, you organize that, dear,' Tabor sighed. 'I'll cover the cost of a chapel and a shack, I mean a hall, for you. Now, is that all?'

'No!' Lucille Langridge rose to say. 'Wouldn't it be better if we devoted our time to helping the less fortunate of these fallen women? We have all seen them around town. Why shouldn't we try to convert them to a decent way of life?'

'I don' theenk you would have much luck at doing that, sweetheart,' Gomez grinned. 'But you are welcome to try.'

The folks sitting on hay bales and barrels in the barn laughingly agreed and began to disperse to their various occupations. 'That's a very good suggestion, dear,' Mrs Tabor called. 'We will have to look into it.'

'Ain't that the sweet l'il thang we saw in the gun shop?' Tex asked, giving an admiring glance at the slim girl in her cotton summer dress of pink candy-stripes and straw sunhat.

'*Sí*, I hope she is as virtuous as she sounds,' Pancho smiled. 'Or she, too, might end up in a home for fallen doves.'

71

'What makes you say that?'

Pancho winked and lowered his voice. 'When I went outside in the early dawn to answer the call of nature I thought I saw her hanging to the back of a young Mexican who came riding down from the mountainside. Maybe I was mistaken.'

'Stranger things have happened.' Tex gave the girl another glance. 'Come on, pal. It's time we bought a pick and shovel and a pack-jack and went looking for silver.'

Pancho groaned at the prospect. 'My back, it already aches at the thought.'

Tex had had the stubble shaved from his jaws in a barber shop, then he and Pancho had visited the Celestial Wash House and clambered into big barrels of hot suds. He had paid Mr Wang two bits extra for a massage, which he found very soothing, especially when his young almond-eyed masseuse stripped off, slipped in naked beside him, and started groping between his knees for the soap.

He felt like a new man as they bought supplies to load on their moke: twelve pounds of oats, flour, salt, coffee beans, and such food stuffs; buckets, ropes, shovels and pick-axes, as well as several sticks of dynamite.

Boom-town prices meant that they were practically broke. Their main outlay, fifty dollars, had gone on the purchase of a mining claim in Shirt Tail Gulch from a jolly gent who persuaded them he had made his pile and was going home to Kansas. He handed over the tattered deed and hurried off to catch the stage, calling out, 'Good luck!'

'Yes, we may need it,' Petersen drawled, wondering gloomily if they might have been sold a pup.

But it was a wonderful day to be in the saddle, the sky brilliant clear blue, the jagged snow-tipped peaks of the Sawatch range to the west towering over them as they ambled on their horses out of Oro City.

Tex had been inclined to call on the gunmaker's older daughter now he was smelling sweeter, but she was, he figured, the kind of feisty dame more interested in a man with a fat wallet in his back pocket, not some wandering cowpoke without a dime. 'Maybe she'll change her mind when I've made my pile.'

They left the gently rounded green valley of the upper Arkansas River and headed into the high hills of the Mosquito range which backed the valley to the east. The snow had been swept clean from its shoulders by the summer melt. It was broad and rolling, more like Scottish moors, cut by steep gulches where most of the mines could be found.

As he rode, Tex studied a tattered, scrawled map which the departing miner had bequeathed, along with the equally tatty deeds to the mine. By dint of several false turns and enquiring of men beavering away at various other claims, they eventually found the Shirt Tail. Not the most exciting prospect: a run-down cabin next to a dark hole disappearing into the hillside.

'First we gotta chop some wood for the stove, get the cabin cleaned up,' Tex said, as he dismounted. 'Then we'll embark on our new career as miners, *amigo.*'

Aristide Luna noisily clattered the gun-shop door closed as he pushed inside, his dark eyes glowering as he met those of Careen. So this was Randall's woman? Her auburn curls accentuated her pale, somewhat severe countenance as she regarded him. 'Yes?' she queried.

The Mexican took his time looking around, removing his riding gloves, a knotted quirt hanging from his wrist. He inspected the rifle racks, his back to her revealing strong buttocks beneath his tight britches and the silver buckled leather *chaparejos.* His spurs glinted viciously.

'Where are your repeaters?' he asked. 'Winchesters?'

'We don't have any.' She was not sure if she had she would want to sell them to him for he bristled hostility like a mongrel dog. But it was true. 'We have ordered a consignment, but they haven't arrived.'

'Oh, yes?' He strode behind the counter and looked beneath it. 'Maybe you are keeping them for your friends.'

'Get back! Who said you could poke about

around here? Why should I lie to you?'

In all probability the Winchesters had arrived but were gathering dust in the luggage depot at the railroad station at Denver or Pueblo. Everybody was clamouring to get freight shipped up through the tortuous passes to this back-of-beyond boom town.

Luxuries like soap, pickles, bolts of cloth, sewing machines, even organs and musical instruments, lager beer from St Louis, Champagne and brandy all the way from France, fancy hats and fashions for ladies were top of the list. The teamsters with their slow-moving bull teams had also to haul mining gear, tools and denim work-clothes, which were much in demand.

No doubt men like Horace Tabor had bribed them handsomely to give preference to his demands for the loads of bricks he needed to build a Victorian-style villa, which would be the first brick edifice in town.

'We've got a British Enfield .303, an excellent rifle, used in the Afghan wars. Or that Springfield single shot,' she said, when he had retreated to his side of the counter.

'I've got one,' Aristide snapped. He picked up the Enfield. 'Heavy load of old junk.'

'If you're looking for long-range accuracy you couldn't do better than that Remington rolling block. Packs a powerful punch.'

'No. How about expanding bullets? You got any?'

'What do you want those for?'

75

'Because I do.' Aristide appraised her shapely bosom beneath the starched grey dress, the fullness of her hips. A lick of lust shivered through him, and he smiled through thin lips. 'You going to sell me anything, or not?'

'You're Rafael's brother, aren't you? Yes, well, I sent him packing the other day, too. It seems we've nothing you fancy so you'd better go.'

'Oh, yes, you've something I fancy,' he said, his dark eyes flickering over her.

Back in the work room it was a hive of activity. One of the apprentices, Amos, was using all his energies to carve a butt-stock in a vice. John Pearce was running an experienced eye along a barrel their other trainee, Ethan, claimed to have straightened. And James Langridge had been making last adjustments to a tricky trigger assembly.

'Behold the Omnipotent!' he exclaimed, brandishing it above his head. 'It's ready for trials.'

Langridge had been renowned in Tennessee for the high quality of his sporting rifles, but muzzle loaders were a thing of the past. So he had obtained the designs of the Winchester '73 and used them to make this, his own ten-shot repeating rifle. He had used Pittsburgh steel for the barrel, although he would have preferred Sheffield, and American walnut for the stock instead of European, but he had to make use of what he could get.

'I've made my own modifications so I don't infringe their patent. What do you think, John?'

Pearce, a master action-filer, inspected the mechanism and said, 'Seems fine.' He held the rifle in both hands. 'The weight's well distributed. Yes, I like it, Jim.'

'Good. What should I ask? A hundred and fifty dollars?'

'Inlay it with gold or silver you might get two hundred. Money seems to be no object these days.'

'I'll show it to Careen,' Jim said, proudly, taking it out to the shop. But when he pushed through the door he saw Aristide standing there, an insolent leer on his face. 'Look! he said. 'My first repeater.'

'A repeating rifle?' the Mexican exclaimed. 'Let me see.'

'No!' Careen shouted, snatching the rifle from her father. 'This is a one-off. It's not for sale.'

'Hand it over, you bitch,' Aristide snarled. 'What you got against me? My gold's as good as anybody's.'

'What's wrong, Careen?' her father asked. 'If he's got a hundred and fifty dollars—'

'I said it's not for sale,' she gritted out, and quickly slipped a .44 into the breech. She raised it, ready for firing and jabbed the rifle at Aristide. 'Get out. You're not welcome here. Any of you.'

'You can't make me—'

'Can't I?' she replied. 'You're trespassing. I'll give you to the count of five then I'll blast you to hell.'

'OK.' Aristide's lip curled back in a mocking leer. 'I'll go. But we'll see who has the last say.'

'What an earth are you playing at, Daughter?'

77

Langridge exclaimed as they watched the Mexican go. 'That's no way to treat a customer.'

Careen kept the Omnipotent held tensely in her hands, 'I don't like him.'

'We need the business. Sam Colt never worried who he sold his guns to, north or south. We need sales. Otherwise we'll starve.'

'There's something evil about that man,' Careen muttered. 'How different can two brothers be?'

EIGHT

'Right, I'll buy you boys a drink before we hit the trail back to the mine,' Captain Randall announced, leading the way into The Golden Garter, one of the biggest and busiest saloons in town.

He had got a remarkably good price for his silver ore from Wells Fargo, buried Mr Callaghan down by the riverside, arranged for a handsome headstone and contacted his kin, bought supplies and paid his men, plus a danger bonus.

'What's it to be?' he asked Rooney, Seamus, his Irish compatriot and a Cornishman, a Londoner and two Poles.

He had furnished them all with weapons, Rooney bagging the Parker shotgun. He paid with silver for their whiskey, vodka and beer and glanced around the crowded establishment. Through a canopy of cigar smoke he suddenly spotted three Mexicans at the far end of the bar, and froze.

'What's the matter, sir?' Rooney asked and, following his gaze, barked out, 'By God, it's them three!'

'No!' The captain tried to stay Rooney's arm as he reached for the shotgun. 'We can't be sure. I don't want trouble in here. Come on, Aaron, let's go.'

But with half-a-tumbler of whiskey inside him Rooney's ire was up. Like an aggressive terrier he pushed through the throng and confronted them. 'You dirty greasers. I know what ye're up to. Come outside. I dare you.'

Aristide Luna was in the middle of talking to Luke Short, his sombrero dangling nonchalantly on his back. He pushed fingers through his dark curls and eyed the diminutive and scruffy Rooney. 'You talking to me, half-pint?'

Short leaning back against the bar, drawled, 'Tell him to go suck the monkey.'

'*Sí*, beat it, gringo,' Raoul growled. 'Pronto.'

The red-haired, snub-nosed foreman, for reply, swung the shotgun, cracking the butt across Raoul's jaw, felling him, then jabbed Jorge in the guts with the business end. 'You gonna fight, you cowardly back-shooter?' he screamed at Aristide.

The saloon had suddenly fallen deathly silent. Aristide's lips curled back in a flashing smile, as if amused by the Irishman. Then his leather boot came up fast and hard into Rooney's crotch.

The Parker exploded, showering a twelve-candle chandelier upon them all, and Rooney dropped the gun as he grovelled on the floor clutching his testicles. Aristide again booted him and raked him with his spur, making him squeal.

Suddenly the whole joint came back to life as waitresses in their skimpy dresses screamed and tried to back away, dropping their trays of glasses, and the rest of Captain Randall's gang rushed to join in the fray.

Soon it was regular free-for-all as burly, drunken miners joined in, swinging their fists wildly at whoever presented themselves and bodies were tossed crashing over tables, or cartwheeled on to the bar.

Captain Randall tried to get to Rooney, but he, too, was socked in the jaw, lost his footing and had to retaliate with fisticuffs. He thrust men aside as he tried to get to his foreman for he could see the little fellow wriggling through the trampling boots intent on retrieving his shotgun.

But there was no stopping Rooney. He grabbed the shotgun again, got up from his knees, groggily, his temper inflamed even more. He fumbled for the trigger of the second barrel and brought the Parker up to fire as Aristide backed away in alarm.

The slightly built Luke Short had not moved his position from the bar. His right hand slid beneath his frock coat to the shoulder-hung Allen and Hopkins .38. It was a movement as fast as a snake's as he brought the revolver out to face Rooney. His bullet blasted out a split-second before Rooney fired. He jumped aside as the Irishman fell backwards and the Parker's hail peppered the back of the bar, smashing glasses on the shelves.

There were more screams and yells as guys and girls dived for cover. They cowered back. And when they looked up Rooney was lying dead in a fast-growing pool of blood, while Luke Short calmly blew down the barrel of his gun and acrid black smoke drifted.

The town mayor, Horace Tabor, had rushed from an upstairs room, and yelled over the landing balustrade, 'What the hell's going on?'

'He fired first,' Short said. 'I was defending myself.'

Horace ran down the stairs and started questioning folk, most of whom agreed Short was the innocent party. Even Captain Randall had to agree that was the case.

'It's contemptible to use a shotgun like that in crowded company,' Tabor announced. 'Aaron Rooney deserved all he got.'

Aristide picked up his fallen companions. 'Come on,' he said, in Spanish. 'We've got another of the bastards. Let's get out of here.'

Horace climbed back up the stairs of the two-storey saloon. Leaning over the handrail of the balcony, a young woman, Baby Doe, had been watching proceedings with interest. In an ankle-length dress of shimmering torquoise satin, with diamonds about her throat and sparkling on her ears, she had a mass of light-brown hair, dreamy blue eyes, and little pouting cupid bow lips.

'Don't worry, darling,' the mayor beamed, 'I've taken care of it.'

Baby had married a ne'er-do-well called Bill Doe and settled in Central City where the appreciative miners called her 'Beautiful Baby'. The name stuck. She had divorced Bill and caught the stage to Oro City, also the eye of Horace Tabor. Suddenly his wealth had made the cantankerous, middle-aged storekeeper an object of sexual attraction to a good chunk of the female population. But Baby lassoed her man and in return he showered her with expensive jewels, dresses and furs.

Horace escorted her back into a private room where two well-turned-out gents were seated in leather armchairs enjoying brandy and cigars at Horace's expense. 'What was all the noise about?' Congressman Clint McCourt asked.

'Aw, a little fracas. Nothing to worry about. Some Irish navvy tried to shotgun a Texan fella, Luke Short. Them Texans are mighty quick on the trigger and Aaron Rooney bought a ticket to the next world.'

'Yes, but what was it all about?' George Johnson, a Republican campaign organizer, demanded.

'Seems Rooney took exception to some Mexicans who were drinking with Short. I blame his boss, Captain Randall, for arming men who can't hold their liquor and ain't a clue how to handle guns.'

'Randall?' McCourt queried. 'That the guy you're trying to buy out?'

'Yes, sir. No hurry. I'll bide my time. He won't last long. He's spent too much time pounding the parade ground to have it up here.' Horace tapped his head. 'I'll get his mine. You'll see.'

The two men, who had made the 120-mile journey from Denver to tap up Horace, exchanged amused glances for the mine owner hadn't struck them as being particularly bright in the brain-box, either.

'Now where were we?' Horace said, seating Baby beside him on a settee. 'You figure you can get me elected a senator if I make a contribution to funds?'

'Hold your horses, Horace,' George grinned. 'Let's take it a step at a time. But you must know money talks. Colorado governor would be the first target. You make us a contribution of eight thousand dollars, or so, you'd be well on your way.'

'Eight? Pah, I'll make it ten thousand as my first token of intent.' Horace went to a desk, dipped a quill pen in ink and scrawled on a piece of foolscap. 'A banker's order to be drawn on Wells Fargo in Denver.'

He grinned through his dangling moustache and waved the paper dry. 'First step on the ladder, Baby. Who knows, no reason why I couldn't become president of the USA.'

Congressman McCourt brandished his cigar. 'Why not? With the right backing the only direction

is up. You couldn't make a worse president than
General Ulysses Grant was, could you? He was just a
damned firewood salesman before the war.'

'President? Oh, Horace, how wonderful!' Baby
Doe cooed in her little girl voice. 'That would make
me first lady.'

'Well, I'd have to get divorced first.'

'True,' George Johnson observed. 'That might be
a small problem.'

'Don't worry, Baby,' Horace said, squeezing the
girl to him. 'You'll always be my first lady.'

Johnson quickly took the banker's order and
tucked it in his wallet, winking at McCourt. 'I'm
getting peckish. Any chance of some grub in this
joint?'

'No problem, gentlemen. I'll have it sent up.
Nothing but the best. Then how about a little game
of stud poker?'

'Why not?' the congressman replied, smiling at
Baby. 'Why not, indeed? That's if you haven't got to
get back to your dear wife?'

'Ough!' Horace gave a grimace of pain as if he
had been struck on his bald head from behind by
some imaginary hand. 'No! She can wait. Augusta
expects me when she sees me.'

'You theenk those bushwhackers will geev us any
problems?' Pancho asked in his broken English, as
he fried an omelette for breakfast on the tin stove in
their shack at Shirt Tail Creek.

'No, why should they? We ain't working for Randall. Nobody's worried about us. That's the way I like it,' Tex replied, as he sat on his bunk and pulled on his boots. 'The only enemy we got to fear is the grizzly.'

'The grizzly bear?' Pancho plonked the wild duck egg omelette on top of a plate of re-fried pinto beans and passed it to him. 'Why should you be so scared of him?'

'You'll know when you see him. Stands eighteen feet tall full grown. You can smell his fiery breath when he roars. You can pump five slugs in his bread-basket and he keeps coming as fast as a race horse. That's why I told ya we got to hang any fresh food up in a tree well away from camp.'

'What eef he smash in here in middle of night? What we gonna do?'

'Shoot him 'tween the eyes and hope you get your shot in first. That's why out in California, when I worked on the Tejon *rancho*, the shepherds used to build a *tepestra*, a platform twelve feet high on stout poles. The grizzly cain't climb a pole but he can git up a tree easy enough.'

'*Amigo*, that's what I do today, build one of those platforms to sleep on.'

'Yeah? Well it'll save me having to listen to you snoring. There's the axe, so while you're doing that you might as well cut down some lodgepoles for pit props.'

'*Sí*, that tunnel into our mine don't look too safe.

86

You theenk we might have a cave in?'

'You can never be too careful when you're going underground.' Tex finished the omelette with relish. 'Very nice. Ain't that coffee pot bubbling yet?'

'Geev it time,' Pancho said, stuffing his own face and licking the plate clean. 'Maybe I shoulda been a chef? Something less dangerous.'

'You won't say that when we're rich.'

'How long will that be, *amigo*?'

'Well, ya never know. I'm willing to give it a good go, but I'd like to get outa here 'fore the winter closes in and the passes git blocked.'

'Ees the winter so bad up here?'

'You're not kiddin', boy. A dozen folk got trapped in a triple avalanche last year. You git caught on the mountains in a bad blizzard, fifty below zero, ye're just as likely to die, or at least lose your toes.'

'*Sí,* but we got a nice warm cabin. Well, it will be when I patch it up.'

Tex got up, poured black coffee from the pot into their tin cups. 'Didn't you hear about that mountain man, Alan Packer, coupla years ago, '74? He an' his mining party of five men got snowed in up in the San Juans. When a rescue party reached 'em the next spring they found Alan sleek and sassy but minus his friends.'

'So', Pancho asked. 'Where were they?'

'Inside Alan. The camp was strewn with well-chawed human bones. Still, at least you got plenty

87

of fat on you if we git in a fix like that.'

'Don' say that,' Pancho protested. 'It not good luck. So what did they do with thees man?'

'He was brought to trial charged with eating up the Democratic majority in Hinsdale county. They didn't hang him, on the grounds he had committed cannibalism not murder. He got forty years.'

Pancho visibly gulped. 'Ain't you got any cheerful stories for me? So, what you gonna do while I axe trees.'

Tex picked up his Winchester. 'I'm goin' hunting, see if I can bag us a nice mule deer.'

He went outside into the brilliant sunshine and saddled his Appaloosa. 'With any luck I should be back by sunset,' he called out. 'I'll be wanting to see some work done, ol' pal.'

NINE

Aristide Luna had recruited two gringos to his band, a lowlife called Zach Sanford, and a surly middle-aged *hombre*, Ben Brown. Zach had tried prospecting but found it too much like hard work, so had taken to mug-hunting. With a sock of lead shot in his hand it was easier to relieve miners of their pokes down dark alleys. Brown, too, was typical gutter trash, a reasonable shot when he was sober, ready to kill any man for the right price.

'You know what to do?' Aristide asked them. 'Stick a pistol in her side and ease her out. Only use force if you have to. I want her alive.'

Maybe his brother, Raphael, had a point. The *Americanos* were in a large majority in this part of the Rockies now. It wouldn't be a good idea to stir up a hornets' nest. They might form a vigilante group, start hanging any Mexican in sight, or even attack and burn down the Buena Vista ranch. He needed to let them think that *Americanos* were behind the attacks on Randall.

So, Careen Langridge was unsuspecting when, basket on her arm, she was doing the morning shopping, calling in Mrs McGinty's pie shop and crossing the entrance to a lane cutting up from the main thoroughfare. Two Americans in scruffy suits and wide-brimmed hats were stood watching the passing cavalcade as even more hopeful prospectors, with their packjacks and wagons rolled into Oro City.

'Hey, sister,' Zach said, taking hold of her arm as she passed them. 'I wanna few words with you.'

'What?' Careen cried with alarm. 'Take your hands off me.'

But an older man, Brown, had caught her other arm and they were pulling her up into the alleyway between the sides of the houses. 'Leave me alone, you oafs,' she screamed, hoping someone would hear her.

Brown clapped a bandanna over her mouth. 'Shuddup,' he shouted. 'Don't give us no trouble.'

Careen began struggling and kicking, wresting one arm free and clouting the older man with the basket. In reply Ben Brown slammed her back against a wall and back-handed her hard across the cheek. 'I said, "Shut it",' he growled. 'I don't want to hurt ya. That's just a start.'

'Come on,' Zach urged, looking behind them, but everybody was intent on their own business and they had, he hoped, been unnoticed. No man wanted to have the killing of a woman laid against them. Not in the West. Men could get sore on that score. 'Let's get her outa here. Slug her again and sling her over the bronc.'

The stinging slap to her cheek had been bad enough, but when Brown hit her again with his full fist it seemed to jolt her head almost from her body and made her senses spin. 'Get up,' he shouted, when he had dragged her to the back of the houses, and lifted her bodily to throw her leg over a saddle. 'Get your feet in the stirrups, you bitch, and sit up straight. You're coming with us.'

Still dazed by the blows, tightly gagged by the filthy bandanna, her wrists tied by rawhide rope to the saddle horn, Careen was led away on the mustang between the two men, who set off at a fast lope, circuiting the back of the town, heading up into the woods beneath the high Sumach range.

Aristide and his *vaqueros* were waiting for them among the pines and he smiled to see the discomfort of the haughty, auburn-haired young woman. He had already scrawled a demand on parchment: *If you want to see Careen Langridge again have the deeds of the Skinned Alive ready to be signed over to us.* As an afterthought he had added, *Plus $1,000 ransom.*

He read it out to them, rolled it up, handed it to Brown. 'Here, take this to Randall. Make sure he knows we're not joking. He hesitates' – Aristide gave a croak as he stroked his thumb across throat – 'she gets it.'

91

'Sure,' Brown muttered, swinging his bronc away. 'What are you goin' to do?'

'We take her up to the old mine. Maybe Randall will have to go into Oro City to get his deeds. Tell him to hurry. We will return to the Skinned Alive at sunset. If he tries any funny stuff it will be the worse for him. And her.'

Ben Brown delivered Aristide's message to Robbie Randall at the Skinned Alive mine. In his shirt sleeves, the captain had been busy – helping his labourers to lower an ore bucket down the shaft. Now that Callaghan and Rooney had gone he had to supervise all the tasks himself. He was trying out a mule-powered winch to hoist the full buckets to the surface again. He wiped the sweat from his face with a bandanna, took a puff at a pipe clenched in his jaws, and eyed the surly thug on horseback.

'Who sent this?' he asked, more shaken than he cared to reveal, brandishing the demand.

'I cain't say,' Brown drawled. 'I'm jest paid to deliver it.'

'Well, I'll be interested to find out when he turns up. But I'm warning you, kidnapping is a hanging offence and if anything happens to that young lady I swear I won't rest until you all dangle by your necks from the nearest tree.'

'That ain't no way to talk,' Brown protested. 'I would advise you to have them deeds all ready to hand over.'

92

He descended the narrow defile and headed back to Oro City. Aristide had given him another errand. He wanted him to call into the gun store and purchase a rifle Langridge had for sale. The $150 cash in gold was burning a hole in Brown's pocket and he was inclined to go wet his whistle in The Golden Garter and double or treble his, or Aristide's money, in a poker game. But by the time he reached Oro City he decided he had better not cross the young Mexican just yet because if Aristide succeeded in getting his hands on the mine there might well be more than $150 in the deal for him.

The younger sister, Lucille, was in the store when he called in and she looked flustered when he said he'd heard about The Omnipotent for sale. There was something about Brown she did not like the look of. 'What do you want it for?' she stalled.

'What ya think I want it for? Hunting, of course.' He slapped the gold coins down on the counter. 'Are you taking my cash or not?'

He watched her closely as she made out a receipt then went to take the rifle from a rack. A nice little piece of muslin. Not so hoity-toity as her sister. Slim of waist and with a neat ankle. Maybe they should think about snatching *her* next time. Old Man Langridge must be worth a dollar or two.

'Thanks,' he said, as she handed him the rifle. 'I'll be seein' ya.'

Brown then made his way over to The Golden

SILVER GALORE

Garter and found Luke Short. 'It's done,' he said. 'We've got her.' He downed a beer and lit a cigar as Luke rolled dice on the bar counter. 'You coming out to Randall's mine tonight?'

'Nope,' Short said. 'I like to stay in the background so nobody knows I'm mixed up in this.'

Brown lowered his voice. 'What's gonna happen to the woman? I don't want her fingering me.'

'She won't, 'Luke replied. 'You'll have to kill her. And Randall, too, once the mine's signed over.'

'Ain't that a bit drastic?'

'We've gotta protect ourselves. Don't tell me you're getting soft-hearted in your old age, Ben.' Luke whistled as he rolled three sixes, and explained. 'They're specially loaded. Everybody's gotta protect their interests. You think I'm in this for peanuts, Ben? No way. You an' me, we're going to be rich. I've been making enquiries. That mine's producing good silver. Why worry about the Mexicans? They're nobodies. The old man's a cripple. There ain't anybody else except Aristide. Once this goes through we'll let him meet with a li'l accident. Then the mine'll be ours.'

He pocketed the dice and grinned. 'Come on, let's go find a couple of gals. Relax, pal. This town's wide open. It's just been waiting for somebody like me to take over.'

When her sister did not get back from her morning shopping, Lucille Langridge began to worry.

94

'Oh, you know what she's like, wilful and head-strong,' her father assured her as he worked in the back room. 'My guess is she's gone out to see Captain Randall at his mine and is in no hurry to get back.'

'But surely she would have let us know,' Lucille replied. 'It's not like her.'

'If she's not back by tea-time we'll ask the mayor to organize a search party. All you have to concentrate on is looking after the store while she is away.'

But Lucille wasn't happy. She was sure something must be wrong. She put on her sunbonnet and made enquiries in the town stores about her sister. 'Sure, she was in here,' Mrs McGinty at the pie shop told her. 'Then I went out to sweep my porch and I saw her across the street talking to two men. They looked to be having a squabble. Then they walked her away up the lane.'

'Why didn't you do something?'

'Sure, it's none of my business what she gets up to. There are so many wild and wayward hussies in this town I can't be going chasing after all of 'em.'

'But my sister isn't wild and wayward.' Lucille left the store and went along to Gomez's corral where Rafael was helping out tending the horses. 'Do you think your brother is involved? He was very threatening to Careen yesterday. She had to make him leave the shop at gunpoint.'

Rafael looked shocked. 'Kidnapping? No, that's impossible. Even Aristide wouldn't be crazy enough to do that.' He remembered his brother boasting to them about killing Harold Callaghan. 'Or would he? Maybe he really has gone loco.'

'What can I do?' she asked, hopelessly.

Rafael strode across to his mare, tightened the saddle girth and swung aboard. 'I will go search through the hills.' He patted his new nickel-plated Smith & Wesson in his sash. 'If Aristide has done this he will no longer be a brother to me.'

Lucille watched him go riding away. 'Oh, dear, poor Rafael,' she groaned. 'It was not fair to ask him.'

When Careen had still not returned by teatime Aunt Becky was having a touch of the vapours, hysterically crying out, 'She always did get into trouble.' Mr Langridge was persuaded to go see the mayor.

'What can I do? I'm a busy man,' Horace told him. 'I sympathize with you, Jim, but Careen is a mature woman. You say the butcher saw her riding off behind town with two men. Well, they were not Mexicans so there's no need to be alarmed. They were probably just escorting her out to see Captain Randall.'

'Can't you get up a search party?' Langridge asked. 'There's thousands of men in this town.'

'Are you crazy? They're *all* too busy. The miners are out at their mines digging away to get what silver they can 'fore the winter comes. The storekeepers, like you, busy selling 'em stuff. And the gamblers

and whores and no-goods hard at it trying to relieve
'em of everything they've got. Nobody's got time to
go gallivanting around the mountains in search of a
foolish girl.'

TEN

All the hectic activity in the gulches around Oro City had scared most of the big game away.

So Tex rode his Appaloosa west, fording the fast-flowing river. The current was strong, but it was not too deep in this smooth glacial valley, and Stan, as he called his mount, went splashing up on to the far bank and bounded away as if both horse and man exulted to be out amid this magnificent scenery.

It did not take long to reach the forest of olive-green boughs, the lodgepole pines that girt the lower slopes beneath the jagged snow-swathed peaks. Here he dismounted, loose-hitched the Appaloosa to a bough, slid the Winchester from the saddle-boot, and muttered, 'I won't be long, old pal. At least, I hope not.'

He started up on foot through the dense wood as silently as he could, trying not to crack any dead branches with his tread. He had caught sight of movement up among the trees above him which with any luck might be a buck and his harem of does. 'Let's hope it ain't bears,' he whispered, as he circled around downwind of whatever it was.

Not that the smaller brown or black bears were much of a threat. They would often be seen busy foraging. They didn't pay much heed to horsemen. But he was not fond of their meat. It was a tad too rich and fatty for his taste. A bear would also have been quite a weight to haul back across the river, whereas he could sling a deer across Stan's hindquarters.

'Ah,' he sighed, as he caught sight of the small bunch. The buck was a fine eight-pointer, probably weighing in at 180 lbs. His head was held proudly erect as he sniffed the air, somehow sensing danger.

Keeping in concealment, Tex stalked closer until he had reached a position fifty yards off and knelt to squint along his carbine's sights as he hugged the Winchester into his shoulder. He waited for the whitetail to move side-on. He wanted to go for a heart-shot, aiming beneath the front leg at the ribcage, but ready to follow wp with lead to the lungs and liver. 'That's better, boy,' he murmured. 'Hold it there.'

But, as Petersen took first pressure on his trigger the buck leapt up the hill as if being attacked by a swarm of hornets and the does streamed away, scrambling through the boles after him.

'What the devil?' What had frightened them? Tex stayed kneeling, listening, and the sound of men's voices, horses blowing, harness jingling, branches breaking as they ploughed up through the wood drifted to him. 'Who the hell?'

The men were calling to each other in shrill Spanish, and Tex caught a glimpse of sombreros, Mexican clothing, and guessed they were just a bunch of *vaqueros* out rounding up stray cattle. He was about to stand up, make himself known to them, when suddenly he saw the girl.

'Careen!' He could not mistake the gunmaker's daughter. She had lost her hat, the sun gleaming on her wild, autumnal-tinted hair. She was dressed in a dove-grey costume and, as Tex ducked down into cover and peered at her, he could now see she was tightly gagged, her wrists bound. There was a look of consternation in her green eyes.

Petersen raised his rifle again, tempted to take out as many as he could. But he hesitated for there were three Mexicans and an American riding closely around Careen. They had reached the point the deer had been and were following on up after them. Fifty yards: easy enough if he fired at the men now to get one or two of them. But what then? Would they grab the young woman to use as a human shield? It was too risky to chance it. Tex released pressure on the trigger and let them go. Then he hurried back down the slope to reach the Appaloosa.

For years these mountains had been a very dangerous place to enter. The Utes would swoop down in venomous raids upon the population. But after a massacre at Pueblo, Captain Kit Carson had led the army in a viciously punitive expedition against them and the Utes' stone-built forts had been blown to atoms by the military's howitzers. Those who survived were herded on to reservations.

Mexican bandits, too, had made the Sangre de Cristo range their stronghold, led by a chieftain named Espinosa, attacking travellers, robbing, raping and seizing females for sale or ransom. They had been routed after Espinosa had been killed by a man called Tobin in Cañon City in the years before the Civil War.

Maybe this gang of desperadoes had decided to revive his bloodthirsty tactics? Petersen had not recognized any of them. Whatever they planned to do with Careen did not bode well for her. He would have to proceed with extreme caution if he were to get her out alive.

Consequently, Tex followed their trail from a safe distance. He did not want to alarm them. By the way they rode along they did not seem to think there was any chance of pursuit. They went charging merrily on for another hour's riding, climbing higher up the mountainside but not yet reaching the top of the tree-line. There were still patches of snow in the shadowy glades in spite of the spring melt. So he had no difficulty in sticking on their tail for hoofprints were clearly embedded amid those of the tracks of snowshoe rabbits and other critters.

Suddenly they had disappeared, apparently descending into a craggy gulch beneath the dark and sombre pines. So Tex reined in his Appaloosa amid the lodgepoles, took his Winchester and carefully climbed down until he could peer from an overhang. What he saw appeared to be an ancient, played-out mineshaft. A narrow stream splashed through the gulch. There was no sign of mining activity but for smoke trickling from the tin chimney of a cabin more dilapidated than his own.

He could hear the sound of laughter and Careen's sudden shrill screams. 'God only knows what they're doing to her,' he muttered. 'I hate to think.'

One of the Mexicans, an older man, had stepped out from the cabin, a rifle in his hands, severe, and shaking his head, as if he might believe in old Spanish courtesy to females and did not approve of what was going on. He was joined by a younger *vaquero*, grinning widely, who sat on a boulder beside him and lit a cigarette.

By now the sun was beginning its fall in the western sky and Tex judged it to be about four o'clock in the afternoon. He was tense and angry and inclined to open fire from his vantage point, but again he had to restrain himself thinking what might happen to Careen if he did.

Suddenly, a tall Mexican strode from the hut. Tex recognized him as the one from Skinned Alive Creek, the one who had killed the engineer. He was followed by the young American, who was fastening his gunbelt and pulling his Stetson down over his brow. They were mounting their horses, the tall one shouting some instructions to the men, probably to guard her well, and setting off back up to the woods.

It was time for Tex to duck down and conceal himself. They passed so close he could hear the creak of saddle leather and jingle of spurs. If they were going back to Oro City they would have a good two hours' ride, Tex thought. They wouldn't be there before sundown. He only hoped they didn't notice his own hoofprints in the patches of snow.

Nor did he want them to hear the reports of gunfire if he attacked. So, he decided to lie low a bit longer. Give them time to get well away for gunshots carried a long way in these mountains.

Gradually the sun dropped behind the sharply outlined peaks towering above them, the snowy crests becoming suffused with a roseate glow. 'Time to play my hand,' Tex muttered.

The two Mexicans had gone back into the shack, one carrying an armful of kindling. With any luck they would be cooking themselves some vittles. So the cowboy clambered down from the overhang, sticking in his bootheels to slide through the scree. When he reached the cabin he did not hesitate. He levered a slug into the Winchester and kicked the door open, charging inside.

The older man, Raoul, stood at the stove, a rag

and pan in his hands. The younger one, Jorge, was sitting on a rickety bunk on which Careen was tied, her face bruised and bloodstained, her dress torn and in disarray. She gave a squeal of alarm as Jorge's right hand snaked towards the revolver in his belt.

'Go on,' Tex taunted, angered by the sight of her. 'Go for it.'

Jorge glanced anxiously around and stayed his hand. 'We did not hurt her, *señor*,' he whined. 'I swear to you.'

But, as he spoke, Raoul hurled the heavy iron pan at the Texan and, as the cowboy was forced to recoil, Jorge took his chance. His revolver was out. The shot crashed, followed by a second from the carbine.

As the acrid gunsmoke curled Careen saw the Texan down on one knee. Jorge clasped his stomach and toppled forward to hit the floor.

'Watch out!' she screamed.

Raoul had reached for his own sixgun, but froze as Petersen spun around, levered another slug into the breech, and faced him. Raoul stared at him, waiting to be blasted apart. Then slowly raised his hands.

Tex was tempted to let the older Mex join his buddy on the floor, but whispered, 'I ain't gonna kill a man I got the drop on.'

He stepped forward, relieved Raoul of his revolver as Careen gasped out, 'That one's not so bad. He tried to stop them.'

Tex stepped back over to Jorge, who was sprawled face down. He fired a bullet into the back of his head and muttered, 'Just making sure. There's many a "dead man" suddenly come back to life.'

He levered the Winchester again and glanced at Careen. She was stretched out, helplessly, her arms tied behind her head to the bunk, one leg attached to a post at the far end, the other hanging free. Her costume had been ripped open, her pale breasts spilling out, and there was the gleam of white thigh flesh above her stocking top. The tall Texan regarded her and drawled, 'A mighty tempting sight.'

'Cut me free,' she begged, her green eyes flashing, angrily. 'Men! You're all the same.'

He grinned, sat on the bunk beside her, pulled his skinning knife and cut her bonds. 'You've been through quite an ordeal. Can you walk? We gotta git outa here.'

'I think so.' She sat up, rubbing at her wrists, and swung her legs to the ground. She stroked her hair from out of her eyes. 'They didn't do anything too bad. Just groped me. But I hate to think what they might do if Robbie gives them the deeds, and they come back.'

'Who's Robbie?' he asked, going back to search Raoul. 'Ah, mighta known you'd have a knife in your boot.'

'Captain Randall. They plan to make him hand over the deeds to his mine in return for my life.

That's where Aristide's gone – to collect.'

'Get on the floor,' he ordered Raoul. 'Face down. I don't trust you. Who's Aristide?'

'The tall Mexican. He's got some embittered idea that the mine belongs to his family.'

Tex took a drink from a goatskin of tequila hanging from a nail in the wall, catching a stream of the fiery liquid in his open mouth. 'Ah,' he breathed out. 'I needed that. You fancy a drop? Put some fire in your veins.'

Careen, too, supped at a trickle from the goatskin. Then she stared at him with her vivid green eyes and suddenly seemed to crumple, putting her arms around his neck and hanging on to him. Tex held her close, sensing the tremors of her body, the wetness of her tears on his shirt.

'Bear up, gal,' he said, gently. 'It's over. We're gonna git you home.'

Careen looked up at him with alarm. 'What about the others? They won't give up.'

'Don't worry. I can handle 'em.'

ELEVEN

Captain Randall was waiting for them as the sun bled away behind the sawtooth peaks of the Sawatch range and the air was suffused with its roseate afterglow. He held his Spencer seven-shot across his chest as he saw the tall Mexican making his way on horseback up through Skinned Alive canyon.

'That's the one who murdered my friend Mr Callaghan,' he muttered to the Cornish miner, Davey Trelawney. 'I'd like to shoot him from the saddle right now. But we've got to take care. He holds the winning cards.'

He had armed his five miners, tried to give them weapons training, but none of them was an expert gunman and Trelawney, for one, had never potted anything but a rabbit before now. Mining was his business. 'Remember, no shooting,' the captain said. 'These weapons are only a bluff, for the moment. Two men dead is quite enough.'

'Don't you worry, sir.' Seamus was holding his

friend the late departed Rooney's shotgun. 'I'm in no hurry to meet my maker. I'll keep my finger off the trigger.'

Aristide gave his lazy, taunting smile when he reached them and glanced at the riff-raff with their guns. Behind him were two Americans. Randall did not recognize them but they looked like the usual murderous flotsam of the frontier.

'So,' Aristide said, without dismounting. 'Have you got the deeds?'

'No, I haven't,' Randall replied in a gruff voice. 'You don't get them until Careen Langridge is safe and sound back in her father's store.'

'He's crazy,' Zach snorted. 'We ain't making the exchange in town for everybody to watch.'

'Gringo,' Aristide shouted, angrily. 'I told you to have the deeds and cash ready for me tonight. What you play at? You want to see the bitch alive again, or not?'

Randall shuddered, involuntarily, at all the remark conjured up. These three looked capable of slitting a throat, man or woman's, at the drop of a hat.

'All right, you bring her here to the mine. To show you I am in earnest I will give you half of the cash you demand and half when the young lady is returned.'

'What about the deeds?' Aristide asked.

'You will have to come into Oro City with me to a lawyer's office. They are in his safe. I will sign them over to you, all legal and above board. You can have the damned mine. You can go your way and I will go mine and not bother you again.'

'How can we trust him?' Ben growled.

'I am an ex-officer and a man of my word,' Randall told them. 'But I warn you, I would not like to be in your shoes if that young lady is harmed in any way by you villains.'

'Villains?' Brown scoffed. 'Listen to him! Who does this old fool, with his army of scarums, think he is?'

'This mine belongs to me and my family,' Aristide shouted. 'Very well. Give me the five hundred. We will be back with her in the morning. I will trust you, *señor*, to do as you say.'

'You had better.' Randall took a leather pouch containing twenty-five golden twenty-dollar pieces from his greatcoat pocket. 'Here.' He tossed it to the Mexican. 'Be sure to be back here with her at dawn.'

Aristide laughed as he weighed the coins in his palm and wheeled his horse away, unaware that Careen was no longer theirs to bargain with. 'Good to do business with you, *Capitan*. Come on, boys, let's go.'

As Randall and the miners watched them depart, Davey muttered, 'I'd rather trust a snake than that Mex.'

'I hope you're not right,' the captain mused.

*

'Where did I leave that darn hoss?' Tex Petersen, on foot, led Careen, riding one of the Mexican's mustangs, up the steep incline away from the old mine. He put two fingers to his lips and gave a shrill whistle. 'Stanley, where are ya?' He heard the Appaloosa snicker. 'Ah, there he goes.'

In spite of her troubles, her aches and pains, Careen could not help smiling. 'Why do you call him Stanley? It's a funny name for a horse.'

'Because I bought him up at Stanley's Stockade from a Shoshone, didn't I, old pal? So he's named after General Stanley,' Tex explained, as he patted the horse's nose and climbed into the saddle. 'You ready for another long ride, gal?'

'I can only try,' Careen had taken the dead Mexican's poncho and pulled it over her torn dress. 'I'm certainly not staying here.'

'Right, let's go. The trouble is I don't want to run into them if they come back, so I'll try an' find a higher route along the top of the tree-line.'

Once the sun had gone it soon grew pitch dark for the moon had yet to rise from behind the high peaks. 'This is too dangerous,' Tex said, dismounting. 'I don't want Stan to break a leg. We'll have to wait a bit.'

The lodgepoles had thinned out as they climbed and a new kind of tree had taken over, majestic spruce that rose as straight as cylinders more than a hundred feet tall. There was a narrow band of them just below the timber-line. 'These are quite something,' he muttered peering up at the branches silhouetted against the night sky. 'How did they git here? I ain't seen the likes since California.'

'They're Engelmanns,' she said, matter-of-factly. 'It's taken them five hundred years to attain that height.'

'You don't say? You seem to be a gal who knows a thing or two.' It was almost too dark to see her face. He found the goatskin and took another slug of tequila. 'Damn,' he said, as he missed the jet and it splashed all over his face. 'You fancy a drop to warm you? We're taking a rest.'

'OK.' She groped in the darkness for the goatskin and found his arm. 'Why not?'

'Why not, indeed?' He reached for his blanket roll and spread it on the soft pine needles. 'Might as well make ourselves comfortable.'

Careen sat with her knees up, chewing on the strip of beef jerky and biscuits he gave her. 'It's all very strange,' she whispered, as she shivered with cold. 'My family will be worrying about where I've gotten to.'

'Yeah,' he muttered, and put an arm around her. 'Why don't ya cosy up aginst me if you're cold? Ya know, body warmth.'

'As long as that's all you're offering.' But she let him draw her gently back on to the soft bed of needles, snuggling up against him as he held his arm around her. It was not an unpleasant sensation. It had been many years since she had known the

111

touch of a man. 'So, how come you were in California?'

'Aw, like the gypsies, I set off wandering from Texas as a boy and didn't stop 'til I reached the Pacific ocean. I worked a while on a *rancho* and headed back agin. I guess I jest got the wanderlust.'

'Haven't you ever fallen for a girl, wanted to put down roots, raise a family?'

'Hell, no.' He gave a snort of laughter. 'You better not git any ideas like that, gal.'

'I wasn't thinking of myself, don't flatter yourself. You're not marriageable material in my book.'

'Not unless I hit it rich? How about this Captain Randall? You stepping out with him? Why should they imagine he would give up his mine for you?'

'Believe it or not, he's in love with me.'

'And what about you?'

'I haven't decided yet.' She lay silent awhile and eventually whispered, 'No, that's not it. The truth is I'm still legally married.'

'You don't say? So where's your husband?'

'Guy? I don't know. Still in Tennessee, I hope. The further he stays from me the better.'

'Like that, was it?'

'Yes.' For some reason she let him hug her into his body. In the darkness she felt a sense of relief, of safety. Whispering to him it was as if she could tell all her secrets, like being in a Roman Catholic confessional. Why was she talking so much? Maybe it was the tequila's effects, but she started telling him about her marriage, about the war, about the soldier she had shot, her arrest, and the Memphis fort commandant, McQuorkindale.

'I was his fancy woman. He had a wife and family back home in the north. I was just his bit of fun. He gave me no alternative. But I was still only fifteen and, in a way, I wanted to be pampered, spoilt like I was as a child. I was sick of the war, of starvation. Of course, our former friends snubbed us. Even Aunt Becky refused to eat any of the luxuries I brought into the house.'

The man holding her made no reply so she went on to tell about how her child, Letitia, had died of the fever in her arms. 'Guy never forgave me. He said it was my fault. But I didn't neglect her. I breast-fed her for three years.'

'If Guy was fighting with Forrest's men how,' Tex asked, 'did he hear about it?'

'Oh, Memphis was occupied by the northerners but messages got through. He roamed around the country with Forrest's advance guard, foraging and spying. He sent a note asking me to meet him out at an old cotton gin on the Mill Road. He wanted me to provide his men with a wagonload of arms.

'So, did you?'

'Yes. Both my father and I had supported the Confederacy. We wanted to help, if we could. And, I suppose we thought if we did it would count in our favour after the war.'

'What happened?'

113

'We drove out in secret in the middle of a night as dark as this, taking the back ways and cane brakes, loaded with rifles, small arms and a ten-pounder Parrott gun. We left the wagon at the gin, mounted our own horses and waited in the woods. Guy and his band arrived. Then suddenly an army patrol charged out of the trees. There was shooting, yells, a hand to hand sabre skirmish. Only Guy and a handful of his men got away. The rest were killed.'

'So, Guy blamed you again?'

'Yes, in his eyes I'd betrayed my own kin, tricked him, set up the ambush. That was a lie. I had no idea how they found out.'

'What about McQuorkindale?'

'He never said a word. But then something strange happened. I fell in love. A young Union lieutenant. Seth. He was at the fort. It was like a thunderbolt. We met secretly. Then one night I looked out of my window and he was in the garden staring up at my window.

'So, you invited him in?'

'Yes, I crept down, unbolted the front door. Of course, we would have chosen that night of all nights.'

'Why?'

'It was the summer of '64. Do you remember, the famous raid on Memphis? Forrest and his men tricked the picket guards, came charging into the heart of the city. Their aim was to capture General Washburn. But, hearing shooting, he escaped from his hotel in his underwear and went running half a mile through the streets for the safety of the fort. McQuorkindale said later it was a hilarious sight, a general in his long johns banging at the gate, begging to be let in. All Forrest captured was the general's uniform which, I might add, he had the good manners to return.'

'So, you were in bed with your beloved lieutenant?'

'Yes, we were woken in the pre-dawn by rebel yells, shooting. And a knocking at the front door. Seth jumped up, pulling on his pants, grabbing his revolver and going out on to the landing. Aunt Becky, with a lighted candle, was opening the door.'

'Guy was making a marital visit?'

'Right. When he saw me in my nightdress beside a bare-chested Federal lieutenant his face contorted with rage. He drew his revolver and started shooting. Seth tried to protect me and fired back. Aunt Becky was screaming. A soldier ran in and grabbed Guy's arm. The town was roused. Forrest and his men were getting out. Guy pointed a finger at me cursing me in the crudest language, and shouted "You whore, I'll kill you one of these days, I swear it".'

'So, he got away, that's the last you saw of him?'

Careen tensed, suddenly feeling the cowboy's hand exploring beneath the poncho to gently cup her bare breast. 'Yes,' she sighed. For some reason she did not repulse him. It felt quite natural, indeed, expected. They were silent for a while, listening to the wind soughing in the branches of the tall trees and noticed that a silver globe of half-moon was creeping out from behind a crag.

'That's why we ran away when the war ended. That's why we left Memphis. That's why I can never contact him. Never marry again.'

'So what happened to your gallant lieutenant?'

'His regiment moved out. He was killed in action at the seige of Nashville. I found his name posted up on the garrison wall among the lists of casualties.'

'Waal, it's quite a story,' he said, turning to her, stroking her cheek, tossing away his hat, his dark hair hanging over his eyes as he stared down at her. 'But I allus figured marriage to be an over-rated institution.'

'You're the first person I've spoken to about these things,' she whispered. 'I suddenly feel as if I'm free.'

He dipped his head to kiss her full lips, long and hard, then murmured, 'You *are* free. You got your life to live.'

Suddenly he rolled on top of her, unbuckling his gunbelt, pulling up her skirts, and Careen could not resist, kissing and caressing, struggling and sighing, drawing him deep into her. Neither could resist the juddering primal urge of life, as old as these mountains, these trees.

TWELVE

Horace Tabor was in high spirits. He had just been offered a million dollars for the rights to his mines. He could hardly believe it as he sat at breakfast in his general store, and studied the cable from a big mining company.

'What's wrong, Horace?' Augusta asked. 'You're not eating your porridge.'

'Nothing, dear.' Horace quickly tucked the cable-gram into his waistcoat pocket. 'Can I have a spoon-ful of molasses on this?'

'We're not made of money, Horace. A pinch of salt is good enough for porridge. You only give me ten dollars for housekeeping.'

Horace always pocketed the store's weekly proceeds, pretending to bank them, and mumbled, 'Why don't you take in lodgers again, Augusta? That way you could keep what you make and wouldn't have to bother me.'

'People keep saying how wealthy we are,

Husband. Surely you could allow me a little more.'

'Ach, you shouldn't pay heed to gossip. All my cash is tied up in other schemes. You don't understand. I'll up your allowance to twelve dollars a week and that's an end to it.'

'Where are you off to now?' his blue-nosed spouse shrilled, as he spooned down his porridge, wiped his moustache clean on the tablecloth and got up to go. 'I hardly ever see you these days.'

Horace was in a hurry to send off a cable to the company's head office in Chicago before they changed their mind. He would hang on to the Matchless, but they were welcome to the others. 'I got investments to make, Augusta. You gotta trust me.'

Horace was also in a hurry to see Baby Doe. He planned to surprise her with a new mink coat and hat in readiness for the Colorado winter. Outside he looked across at the chimneys of his smelting works on Fryer's Hill emitting their gritty smoke. Yes, you had to think big in mining. Big machinery. Big development. The business sharks had smelt money and were quickly moving in. The hills were teeming with thousands of men from all walks of life trying to make their fortunes with their small mines. Sure, they were sifting plenty of silver from the blue clay and the US Treasury was glad to buy it. Each month they used four million ounces of silver for the country's coins. But the small men, the lone operators, would soon be elbowed out, swallowed up by the big sharks.

Baby Doe was also planning a surprise. Tattooing was the current fad among ladies, upper or lower crust, and she was sitting in Mr Needles' chair, her mid-parts exposed as he brandished his instrument. A discreet part of the anatomy, buttocks, shoulder or arm, were generally preferred, but Horace had given her such a wonderful time, provided their lovely love nest above The Golden Garter, that Baby had decreed Mr Needles should perform his art on the pale skin just above her own love nest.

'Ouch, that hurts,' Baby cried.

'It'll hurt a lot more if you want it removed,' the tattooist and wigmaker replied, as he imbued her with an entwined, 'H&B, Love Is For Ever'.

He extracted $200 in cash payment from Baby, swished a curtain back and called out to a bevy of goodtime girls in his waiting-room, 'Right, who's next?'

Horace had checked out how work was proceeding on the brick, Victorian-style villa he was building on the edge of town, and the three-tier music hall in the centre. Like his wife he wanted to bring a little culture to Oro City, but his taste was for the more vulgar variety.

Then, with his parcels under his arm, he stepped into the Garter and called for his morning snifter before he went upstairs. He noticed Luke Short sitting in a corner with a couple of ne'er-do-wells, Zach Sandford and Ben Brown, as well as Aristide and one of his *vaqueros*.

Well, if he was taking his ease in here, the Mexican couldn't be responsible for the disappearance of Careen, as James Langridge was claiming, could he?

The truth was that Aristide had returned to the old mine for Careen, found her missing, Jorge dead, and Raoul trussed up like a roasted chicken. They had come into town at first light of dawn, surrounded the gun store and gone storming in, kicking open doors of the sleeping quarters to search for her, ignoring Aunt Becky's screams, Langridge's imprecations, and Lucille's demands to know what they had done with her sister.

'We don' know nothin' about her,' Aristide replied, impassively. 'We ain't got her. She's been kidnapped.'

'Yeah,' Brown growled, his revolver at the ready. 'We're just checking up she ain't here.'

'This is crazy,' Lucille said, when they had gone. 'If they haven't got her, who has?'

'I'll drive out to see Cap'n Randall,' her father promised. 'See if he knows anything.'

'I'm coming with you,' Lucille cried.

All Aristide knew was that the interfering Texan had taken her. But where to?

'Do I have to do everything for you?' Luke sighed. 'He's got a mine someplace. You can find out where at the Mining Institute. Do that, then go get him. And the girl. Carry on as before.'

He watched them go and muttered, 'Seems like

I'm surrounded by incompetents. Maybe I oughta take care of that Texan myself.'

In his sons' absence Demetrio Luna had his remaining *vaqueros*, six of them, scour the mountainsides in a wild-riding round-up of his longhorns. It was time to take them into Oro City where prime beef was fetching top prices. Word had also reached him that Jorge had been killed in a bungled attempt by Aristide to kidnap some white woman.

'It is time I went down there to take over,' he shouted at his wife as he was lifted from his wheelchair, and hoisted into the air by a rope slung over a rafter in the barn and sat in his saddle. 'Before that fool son of mine gets hisself killed, too.'

'Please, Demetrio,' his wife screamed, 'be careful. Those gringos are as crafty as wolves.'

'Don't worry, woman.' The old man's paralysed legs were tied into the stirrups. 'It feels good to be in the saddle again.' He cracked his bullwhip and set his mustang leaping forward. 'Follow me, *muchachos.*'

His hatred for the man who had stolen his mine burned steadily in him as he rode down to the valley and towards Oro City. Jorge had been a fine young man. Maybe there would be more casualties. But he had had enough of watching helplessly from a wheelchair. He would show the gringos that it was not advisable to cross *Don* Demetrio del Hasta de

Luna whose ancestors had been brave *conquistadores*.

When he and his men galloped into Oro City, corralled and quickly sold the steers, *Don* Demetrio found Aristide about to set off in search of the Texan's mine, accompanied by Raoul, Zach and Ben, and several ruffians they had recruited in Rosie's saloon.

But as they moved off out of town they were confronted by Raphael, who was about to call at the gunstore to see Lucille and report that he had had no luck in his search for her sister. 'What are you doing here, Father?' he cried. 'Where are you all going?'

'What are *you* doing here is more to the point?' *Don* Demetrio shouted, hauling his feisty mustang to a halt. 'Are you riding with us, or not?'

'Why,' Raphael asked. 'What's happened?'

'That lousy Texan, Petersen, has kidnapped the gunmaker's daughter,' Aristide put in. 'We are riding to rescue her.'

'That's a lie,' his brother cried out. 'You're crazy. You're the one who stole her away; I'm sure of that.'

'Get out of the way, you whelp,' *Don* Demetrio sent his whip to snap at his son's face. 'I warn you, you are either with us, or against us. If you are against us you are no son of mine.'

'You've got it all wrong, Father.' Raphael backed his mare away and raised his arm to protect his face from the stinging lead-tipped whip. 'Please, I beg you, forget this foolishness. It can only mean blood-shed.'

'The bloodier the holier,' one of the *vaqueros* yelled. 'Come on, *señor*, let's go.'

'The Texan's asking for a tight necktie,' Ben hollered. 'And he's gonna get it. That's the price for any man who steals and rapes a young woman. I bet he's got her in his cabin right now. What do you say, boys?'

'Yeah,' one of the men he'd found in the saloon yelled. 'Let's go get him.'

'There's a twenty-dollar cartwheel for the man who takes him,' Aristide said. 'Get out of the way, Raphael, you coward. Or do I have to shoot you down?'

'Stay where you are, men.' Raphael raised his hand, manoeuvring Maria to block their way. 'You've got it all wrong.'

'You've asked for it.' Aristide pulled a Remington revolver from his gunbelt, levelling it at him. 'I'm sick of you, you milksop.'

A look of disbelief crossed Raphael's face. 'You wouldn't?' But the darkness in his brother's eyes told him he had better get his new Smith & Wesson out quick. As he did so Aristide fired and a searing pain in his arm made Raphael drop the nickel-plated revolver. '*Aagh!*' he cried.

Aristide grinned, and spurred his big mustang forward to ram the mare, Maria, in the side, toppling her over. She screamed and kicked as she hit the ground, trapping one of her rider's legs beneath her.

'You asked for that,' Demetrio Luna shouted, and charged forward cracking his whip. 'Onwards!'

As the posse dashed after him Lucille ran forward and tried to pull the agonized Raphael away from the mare as she struggled to her feet.

'He's in a bad way,' James Langridge said. 'Looks like his leg's broken. And his arm's a mess. Let's take him into the house.'

'Phew!' Tex sat up on the bunk. 'I musta been fagged out. All that ridin'.' He grinned at Careen who was lying beside him, lazily blinking her eyes. 'How long we been asleep?'

They had arrived at the Shirt Tail mine about four in the morning. He had planned to stay awake, keep on guard, but she had caught hold of him, pulled him down on the rickety bunk beside her. 'Well,' he had said,' we should be safer here than at your gunshop. Nobody much knows I've taken this claim.'

So, they had gradually drifted into sleep in each other's arms. Now the sun was up and he guessed it must be about nine o'clock, if not later. 'I didn't kill no fresh meat, so I guess it's gonna have to be salt bacon for breakfast.'

He pulled on his boots and stood to rekindle the tin stove and put the coffee pot on to boil. He opened the cabin door and peered out. There was no sign of life apart from a jay hopping about. 'If you wanna wash or whatever, you can go down by the stream, Careen.'

It sounded strange saying her name for the first time, stranger still this sudden intimacy that they shared. He checked his Winchester and propped it handy, then set to frying up some bacon and eggs. 'Breakfast won't be long,' he, when she returned, her wind-tangled hair combed. She had washed and was looking refreshed, apart from the bruise about her eye.

'You got a nice shiner,' he said, pulling her to him and kissing her pale, high-cheekboned face, her soft, full lips. 'I bet you were a li'l minx in your younger days.'

'The bacon's burning,' she reminded him. 'And I'm not that old. Not much older than you.' She watched him tending the food. 'You've certainly made me feel young again.'

'How you like 'em. Sunny side up?'

'Yes, please. I'm starving. What are we going to do?'

'I dunno,' he said, passing the thick slice of bacon and egg to her on a tin plate, He made his own meal and ate in silence, sitting on the bunk. 'I sure don't know.'

When they had finished eating, and supped some hot coffee, Careen stretched her shapely legs out on the bunk. 'Do you believe in love at first sight?' she asked, studying him.

'Waal, it sure saves a lot of time.' He met her amber flecked eyes and smiled. 'I never was keen on all that courtin'.'

'Or was it just—?'

'Lust?' He rolled a cigarette deftly and lit up. 'Maybe a bit of both. What you gonna do about the captain?'

'I don't know.'

'You don't see much future with – what was it you called me – a charbroiled vagrant?'

'I'm sick of poverty, of running, that's all. I'd like to live a decent, civilized life again. You said yourself you're a drifter.'

'Yes,' he sighed, 'just like the tumbling tumble-weed. I wonder what's happened to that pal of mine, Pancho? There's no sign of him. I guess the lazy varmint headed into town when I didn't return. He's got a pash for Fat Rosie.'

Careen laughed. 'Everybody's got these crazy passions. We're not the only ones.'

'Waal, it was good under them trees—' Tex stopped, raising a finger, listening. He thought he had heard the whinny of horses. 'Stay put. I think we've got visitors.'

Aristide and his comrades dismounted as they reached the Shirt Tail, all except his father, who stayed in the saddle, unable to get down. 'Check they're not in the mine,' he snapped, and rode his horse forward until he was about fifty yards from the shack. Woodsmoke was trickling from the tin chimney. 'I know they're in there,' he said, drawing a brace of Navy sixes from his belt, holding them, ready-cocked, one in each hand. 'Spread your men out around the hillside, Aristide. Tell them to take cover.'

As his son signalled to the Anglos and Latinos to do so, and they scrambled to find a good position, *Don* Demetrio bellowed, 'Send the gal out and throw down your guns. You're surrounded, Texan. You've got no chance.'

Aristide grinned, hugging his Omnipotent into his shoulder and taking a bead on the cabin. He had been longing to test it out. Ten slugs in the mag. Like his father said, they had no chance.

Inside the cabin Careen hissed, 'I'm not going.'

'Go, save yourself.'

'No. They'll kill me once they've got their hands on the captain's mine. I know too much.'

She was hanging on to the bunkhead and Tex saw from the determined look on her face that she would not change her mind. At least not yet. 'Get on the floor then. Stay low. All hell's gonna break loose in a few seconds.'

He twitched aside a ragged hide covering the cabin window and poked out his Winchester, peering out. A stoutly built old man, a Mexican, was sitting on his horse. He could have blasted him to Kingdom Come, but it just didn't seem right.

'*Señor*,' he shouted. 'Call your men off. You are

making a big mistake. The young lady ain't leaving here. Nor am I. Dincha see the sign?'

'What sign?' Luna asked.

'Claim jumpers will be shot.' Tex fired and the old man's sombrero was torn from his head. 'You've been warned.'

At that Luna gave a yell of fury and started blasting away with both pistols.

Tex ducked down. 'Whee!' he whistled. 'He ain't a bad shot.'

He, too, hit the deck, covering Careen with his body as the expected onslaught began. Every man out there began lambasting the cabin with carbines, rifles and revolvers. It was like a hurricane of hailstones hitting the cabin's log walls, splintering the door and windows, showering them with shards.

'*Boom*!' The Omnipotent roared with a flash of flame as a slug powered out and smashed through one of the walls, whistling over their heads and embedding itself in the far wall. Aristide yelped with joy as he pumped shot after shot into the cabin until the ten in the magazine were spent. He clutched the smoking carbine to him. Nobody could survive that onslaught.

The other men ceased firing and Ben Brown climbed to his feet and peered over a rock. The echoes of the shooting bounced away off the ravine walls and there was a sudden silence. 'I think we got him,' he shouted.

They were his last words as a bullet from Tex's Winchester whined and went clean through his chest. Brown went slithering down the slope, blood pumping from his chest.

Tex did not cease the fusillade. *Pow! Pow! Pow!* Shot after shot rang out as he picked his targets, pumping the Winchester, two more men screaming as they were hit. But he was now out of lead as he dropped back, seeking a box of bullets. It would take at least twenty seconds to reload.

The attackers took their chance, sending another concerted volley at the shack, several abandoning cover and charging closer to get a good shot in.

As they did so to their surprise a carbine cracked out from above them and one of the town pariahs was flattened with a ball of lead in his back. He groaned, 'I'm hit!', stating the obvious as he always had, before he died.

Zach spun round and looked up at a contraption of planks suspended on four lodgepole legs from where the shot had come. He saw a burly man in a sombrero peering over. But he was too late. Pancho's bullet hit him between the eyes.

'All right,' Careen screamed. 'Hold your fire. I'm coming out.'

The men closing in on the cabin paused as the young woman edged out of the door. Her eyes wild, she was wrapped in a poncho. All watched her. But suddenly she brought out a Colt Peacemaker, and took deliberate aim, fanning the hammer, cutting down first one man, then another, Mexicans and Anglos, whoever presented themselves, backing back into the cabin as her six were spent.

'Jeez,' Tex breathed out. 'Howja learn to shoot like that?'

Careen grinned at him and squatted down to reload the dead Jorge's smoking gun. She was glad she had brought it along. 'That gave them something to think about.'

The normally peace-loving Pancho's blood was up. He had enjoyed a pleasant night's sleep on his new *tepestra* only to have been rudely awakened by these intruders. As Tex said, they must have seen his scrawled sign.

He peeped over the platform and took aim again. The old man on the horse was asking for it. So he let him have it. Luna slumped forward, hanging on to the horse's neck as it started away. Aristide leaped forward to grab the bridle and support his father, presenting a clear target. So Pancho pumped out a shot from his carbine at him. Blood spurted from the tall Mexican's upper arm and his face twisted with agony. He raised the Omnipotent to reply but was knocked off his feet by the sudden blast of an explosion.

Tex had lit a stick of dynamite, fanned the fuse, and tossed it out of the window. Unluckily for Pancho his throw was not good and the dynamite landed at the foot of his sleeping tower. As flames roared and rocks flew in all directions the *tepestra* tumbled to one side and Pancho was pitched from his perch, his face registering horror as the ground rose to greet him. He hit it hard as boulders tumbled on top of him.

Inside the cabin Tex was busy lighting another stick, as Careen nimbly filled his Winchester's magazine for him. He knelt up and slung the dynamite towards a town no-good who was taking aim with a rifle at them, then dropped back into cover as rocks and bodies were blown to smithereens.

'You think they've had a bellyful?' he asked, as it went strangely silent again outside. 'I'll take a look.'

The scene of carnage that greeted him was not to his taste. Dusty and bloodily injured men were pulling themselves out of the rubble. Aristide was hanging on to his father's reins, leading his mustang away. He turned and pointed a finger, his face twisted with pain and fury. 'You win this time, gringo. But I'll be back.'

The older *vaquero*, Raoul, met Tex's eyes. He grinned and stuffed his long-barrelled revolver into his sash. He raised a finger to his sombrero to salute him, as if to say, 'You put up a good fight'. Then turned and helped a comrade to go limping back to his horse.

'There they go, their tails between their legs,' Tex said, as they watched the rest of the posse and the walking wounded hurry away after them. He hugged Careen into him. 'It should be safe for you to go home now. I don't believe they'll pull that stunt again.'

'What are you gonna do about the dead ones?'

'Aw, the coyotes and ravens'll soon pick 'em clean. I'll keep their cash. You can have the guns. To the winner the spoils. Need somethang for my trouble.'

Suddenly, he heard a plaintive, 'Help me!' coming from beneath a pile of rubble. Tex hauled the rocks away and scrabbled at the dirt. Pancho's face appeared, spitting out dust. 'What you try to do, *amigo*, kill me?'

'I wondered where you'd gotten to,' the cowboy drawled as he hauled him out of the dynamited crater. 'Hey, hang on a minute! What's all this?'

He knelt and ran his fingers through a seam of blue sludge that had been unearthed, thrilled to see a silvery sparkle. 'Pancho, ol' pal, I figure the guy who sold us this claim was diggin' in the wrong place.'

'I think you're on to something,' Careen said, excited, too. 'You could end up as rich as Horace Tabor.'

'Waal,' he drawled. 'We'll see.'

He climbed out of the crater and came face to face with Captain Randall, on Rajah, as he rode up out of the creek. He had a Colt in his fist and shouted, angrily, 'All right, put your hands up. If you've harmed Careen you're a dead man.'

132

'Don't be ridiculous, Robbie,' Careen smiled, as she joined them. 'Put that gun away. Mr Petersen rescued me.'

THIRTEEN

Soon the short summer passed and winter snows swathed the mountain slopes with their mantle; skeins of honking geese headed south, and the hills resounded to the bugling of elks, the clash of antlers as the bucks began their rut. Tex and Pancho caulked the cracks in their hut's walls with clay and moss and dug in. The nights became so brittle cold they almost hugged the stove. Their new shaft was producing paydirt. Tex had acquired a horse sleigh and he hauled their loads into town, his Appaloosa stud floundering through the drifts. It was back-breaking work but proving worth it.

'We ain't rich, but we ain't poor, either,' he told Careen when, wrapped in a bearskin coat, he called in before Christmas to stock up on copper-jacketed cartridges. 'Let's put it that way.'

She was friendly, but distant. When he asked her to join him for a meal or a drink over at the saloon, she shook her head. 'I've been stepping out with

Captain Randall. I don't think I ought.'

'Have you told him yet?'

'My history? About Guy? Yes, I have.'

'How about us?'

'No.' She smiled radiantly for a moment. 'I thought I'd skip that bit.'

So, it was just one of those flings, a night of madness, according to Careen, she had best forget. 'I guess I ain't eligible enough a bachelor yet,' he said, with a touch of bitterness.

In the town he bumped into Rafael. The Mexican youth had been laid up for six weeks as his broken leg healed, nursed by Lucille. News had reached him from his ranch that his father was still alive, recovered from a bullet wound in his side. His brother Aristide had, apparently, disappeared, but was believed to have headed for Denver. Rafael himself, was helping Gomez buy and sell horses.

Mexicans were no longer popular in Oro City after the scandal of Careen's kidnap got out. In fact, many saloons and stores had put up signs: 'No greasers or Indians'. Horace Tabor had called a public meeting to propose that the town no longer needed a Spanish connotation and its name should be changed to the more solidly American Leadville in honour of the carbonate of lead containing the silver through which it had become rich. This was riotously approved.

Horace had gained another million dollars by investing in the public corporation that bought up his mines, shares springing from $5 to $30 in no time. He celebrated by buying Baby Doe an unofficial 'engagement' present – a $100,000 diamond necklace.

In fact, he was constantly in the news, as was his girlfriend; an article in the *Rocky Mountain News* lauding her as 'without doubt the handsomest woman in Colorado', and comparing her body and bust to that of Venus.

His contributions to Republican funds, totalling $200,000 by now, and his donations to churches and charities paid off. In the new year he was elected lieutenant governor of Colorado. He built himself a magnificent mansion in Denver, with a 100 peacocks roaming the front lawn, installed Baby Doe in a villa in Leadville, campaigned for the Denver and Rio Grande railroad to extend its line to Leadville, and sent away as far as France, Italy and Japan for marble and fine furnishings for the opera house that was his pet scheme.

Some considered that he was a walrus-moustached bumpkin, an innocent in the world of high finance, and that his empire was not well-glued together. But it did not bother Horace. The next step on his ladder was to try to become a senator and then take his seat in the White House.

Meanwhile, the bony-faced Augusta turned a blind eye, refused to act the lady in Horace's grand house and worked resolutely on in her post office and store.

As for the new named Leadville, its reputation as the dirtiest, noisiest, roughest, sweatiest, smelliest city in the West just grew and grew. There were now 20,000 mines, eighty-two saloons, and thirty-five bordellos. Drunkeness, gaming and debauchery never ceased, by day or night.

'It sure is a rootin'-tootin' town,' Pancho yelled, as he and Tex made their way along the icy side-walks to reach Fat Rosie's. She, at least, had put no ban on Latinos. And with their pokes of silver they were made royally welcome. In fact, as the winter wore on they were more often to be found there than out at the mine.

It was a place of warmth and gaiety where the roulette wheels spun and the barleycorn flowed.

They were a mixed bunch, indeed, who congre-gated in the saloon. Not just gamblers, whores, bunco operators, mountain men and miners, but tinhorns arrived from the East and purveyors of quack medicines, like 'Doctor' Charles Broadbent, who was busy selling dandelion pills for dyspepsia, 'inhaling balm' for catarrh and rheumatism, and bottles of his 'Great Remedy' to cure 'loss of memory, lassitude, nocturnal emissions, noises in the head, dimness of vision and aversion to society'.

'Maybe I oughta have a bottle of that,' Tex yelled to Pancho above the din, the whiskey making him loquacious.

'That magnetic silver detection machine that other fella's sellin' might be more use to us, *amigo*,' replied Pancho, tipping back a bottle of tequila by the neck.

Millionaires and muckers rubbed shoulders. Men like Tom Welsh, of Tipperary, who had found an abandoned mine and made $75,000 in two months. He was busy spending it at the blackjack table. Ten years later Tom, with the luck of the Irish, would develop another such mine which would yield him seven million dollars.

'Why don' you saddle-up a woman, *amigo?*' Pancho asked as they got stuck into a bottle of bourbon. 'Why you let that gunmaker's filly get away?'

'Aw, she's got a bad case of the respectables,' Tex replied. 'She wants to be somebody. The captain's more her sort. I wish her the best of luck.'

'So, there's plenty more dames.' The Mexican waved his hand airily at a bunch of screaming dancing girls up on the podium. 'Take your choice.'

'I've no hankering to piss pins and needles,' Tex muttered, for gonorrhea was rife among such women. He winced at the cacophony of cat-screeching fiddle, honky tonk piano and the general bedlam in the bar. 'Maybe I'll go let Chinese Sally ease my oysters in the Celestial Bath House.'

'I got an appointment upstairs,' Pancho beamed, going across to Rosie, who was perched on a stool beside the bar. 'She's sweeter than a posy.'

Tex watched him slip her a poke of silver, and smiled as they climbed to the landing and her private room, both their large bottoms wobbling.

'They make a fine couple.'

Bucktooth Alice, in a velvet dress tighter than an eel's skin, and her pet squirrel on her knee, taking a break from her horizontal labours, had joined him. Tex tipped bourbon into her glass. 'Keep that critter away from me. He looks dangerous.' Tex eyed the ceiling apprehensively. It had begun to creak and reverberate. 'One of these days them two are gonna come crashing through on top of us.'

Alice stroked the squirrel, which looked anxious to take a leap at him. 'How about it, Tex? It's half-price to you.'

'I ain't in the mood,' he growled, easing the hogleg Peacemaker hanging on his hip for who had swaggered into the bar but Aristide Luna, accompanied by the dapper little Luke Short. 'Waal, look what's crawled outa the sewer.'

Aristide heard the remark and turned to him with a snarl of hatred. 'Ah, if it isn't the interfering Texan.' His hand slid towards his own revolver. 'You lookin' to feenish it, gringo?'

'You can go kiss my granny's black cat's hairy backside,' Tex replied, raising his glass.

The saloon had dropped suddenly quiet, but there was a burst of laughter at Petersen's remark. 'Come on.' Short caught hold of Aristide's arm and pushed through to the bar. 'Don't start nuthin', you might git lynched.'

'That bastard insulted me. You heard him,'

Aristide hissed. 'When are you going to kill him and Randall?'

'When I git the rest of the cash you promised me.'

Aristide dashed back a glass of tequila, scowling at the men in the bar. 'OK,' he said, taking a pouch of gold coins from his jacket. 'Here is three hundred. Now you owe me.'

Short tucked the cash in his pocket and smiled as he looked across at Petersen. 'Consider it done. He's a dead man.'

Captain Randall had, frankly, been shocked by Careen's revelations of her past, especially the part about McQuorkindale, about her being both his and Seth's mistress. He, himself, was an officer and gentleman of the old school. 'I guess people have to do all sorts of things they wouldn't normally do to survive a war,' he excused her. 'But I think you must write to your husband's attorneys. I can't believe he holds such a grudge against you after all this time. He would probably be glad to be free to remarry, himself.'

'You don't know Guy.'

But Careen had accepted the captain's proposal of marriage and it was obvious she must seek a divorce. 'I'll attend to it, Robbie. I'm determined now.'

Ignoring the disgraceful shenanigans going on all about them, the hardcore of Christian folk supported activities to improve people's minds like Augusta Tabor's Belle Esprit Society. The captain escorted Careen to talks about the Seven Wonders of the World, piano performances and singing recitals at her new meeting hall.

Mr Tabor had paid to have the first of what would be eight new churches erected – a small price to pay to keep his wife out of his hair, what was left of it. And his new music hall was to have a grand opening.

Baby Doe was, in fact, the main attraction, in a headdress of ostrich feathers, high button shoes, white kid gloves to the elbows, sparkling with diamonds and pearls, and in a dress of lavender silk cinched in tighter than a rodeo horse, ultra-décolletée both front and back.

There was a gasp of amazement as she and Horace stepped into their box and he removed her ermine wrap to reveal all. The gawpers in the three tiers of seats whistled and cheered as *Macbeth* began. Much abbreviated, the accent was on witches, stabbings and severed heads, with breaks for skimpily clad dancing girls and a trapeze act to keep the miners in the stand-up stalls happy.

'Appalling,' the captain chuntered. 'What a vulgar travesty of art.'

If secretly amused, Careen had to agree. Over supper afterwards she told him Guy's attorneys had replied. There was no objection to a divorce which could be arranged quickly. 'We could be married in the spring, Robbie.'

'Good. I'll inform my family and make the preparations,' he said, as she kissed him goodnight. 'By the way, how is young Rafael?'

'He's fine. Lucille is crazy in love. I've given up trying to keep them apart. Only he doesn't have much of a future. He's bought a string of mules and is felling lodgepole pines, selling them to the mines for pitprops.'

'At least that shows enterprise. I like the lad, and as Lucille will shortly be my sister-in-law I've been thinking, maybe I could take him into my mining business, show him the ropes.'

Careen appeared doubtful. 'I'm not sure that's a good idea. There's all this bad blood with his family.'

'That's what I mean. To tell the truth I've been feeling a a tad guilty. The Skinned Alive used to be their mine after all. Perhaps this way we could build bridges.

'But what about his brother? You know what he's like. For God's sake, Robbie, he all but raped me. He's crazy.'

'Come on, my dear. We must forgive and forget. Perhaps,' he mused, 'we could have a double wedding, Rafael and Lucille and you and me.'

'Perhaps.'

FOURTEEN

Leadville was strung with banners and bunting across the main street as Horace Tabor drummed up votes for his Republican nomination. He had hired a marching band to lead his open carriage, drawn by four greys. Trestle tables had been set up outdoors laden with hams, joints of beef, oysters and salmon cooled in blocks of ice brought down from the lakes where it froze twenty feet deep. There were barrels of beer and whiskey, free to all. So folks went wild as Horace harangued them. 'I'm a man of the people, a mining man,' he bellowed through a megaphone. 'Vote for Horace Tabor.'

His fortune was now close to nine million dollars so he could afford to be generous. He just couldn't seem to stop making money, speculating in coal, water, banks, lumber, and trying to corner the market in wheat.

He had spent $750,000 on his opera house and on the day it opened an audience of 1,500 rose to give him a standing ovation. Horace was in seventh heaven.

However, significantly, not among the audience was the dour and flinty Augusta Tabor. She could no longer refuse to confront the humiliations poured upon her and had sued for divorce.

Horace, in a penguin suit and Lincoln hat, with a diamond stickpin in his cravat, pushed through the throng, shaking hands and kissing babies, to climb the steps into the newly built Clarendon Hotel, the most luxurious establishment in town, with a chef imported from Delmonico's in New York City.

The Colorado legislature, meeting in Denver, was to elect two senators, one for a full term, the other to fill a vacancy lasting only thirty days. Lieutenant Governor Tabor had pulled every string possible and was confident of getting the full term in Washington.

He beamed through his magnificent moustache as he saw Congressman Clint McCourt awaiting him for a celebratory luncheon. But McCourt did not look too happy and was beckoning him into a private room.

There they found George Johnson amid a spread of newspapers from various cities of the US. 'You're in the shit, Horace. The Press are on to you and when those hounds get their teeth in the back of your pants it's bad news, boy.'

'Look at this!' McCourt gruffly jabbed a finger at a banner headline of the *Chicago Examiner*. MISERLY

MULTI-MILLIONAIRE'S WIFE'S LIFE OF POVERTY

He began to read aloud: 'The hard-working Augusta Tabor was forced to take in boarders to make ends meet while horrible Horace showered his blonde, cherub-faced beauty, Baby Doe, with diamonds and furs. . . .'

The judge granting the divorce settled $300,000 on Augusta, which, the paper pointed out, was three months pocket money to Horace. Every news-paper took the same tack. 'This poor woman who had devotedly supported her husband through thick and thin was cast aside as soon as Tabor hit the bigtime. Today he has the bare-faced gall to try to buy his way into the senate,' fulminated the *Examiner*.

Much of Horace's $200,000 donations to Republican funds had found its way into McCourt and Johnson's personal bank accounts. 'It's no good, Horace. We've tried our best for you,' the congressman said, 'but the party high-ups feel your marital misadventures won't sit well with the voters.'

'So?' Horace looked perplexed. 'What does that mean?'

'It means you're only gonna get the thirty-day term,' Johnson replied. And McCourt added, 'It means you ain't never gonna be president.'

Horace sat down, blinking back tears. 'But . . . but you said—'

'Sorry, old pal.' McCourt patted him on his shiny dome. 'You cain't have your cake and eat it. Which reminds me, let's go git a drink and some grub.'

So, Horace got his thirty days in Washington, and while he was there married Baby Doe, who was decked out in a $1,000 wedding dress. Then they returned to Denver and Leadville to astound every-body with their opulent life-style. The dour Augusta retired discreetly back to New England.

The icicles were dripping from the eaves, the snow on the valley slopes was melting, the thaw setting in, when two miners who had not made a mint like Tabor decided to quit. Tex stuck his shovel in a pile of scree and said, 'Whoever takes over is welcome to it.'

The Shirt Tail had given them a good return on their fifty-dollar stake, but it was never high-grade ore and now they had hit a wall of solid rock. 'Mining, you can keep it,' Tex drawled. 'I'm tired of being stuck down that dark hole.'

'What you gonna do, *amigo*?'

'I got ten thou' stashed in the bank. I'm headin' up to Miles City, Montana, claim me a good stretch of land the Sioux ain't in need of no more now they're on the reservations. I'll build me a house and stock it with best Herefords.'

'Ten thou'!'Pancho gave a whistle of awe. 'How you manage to hang on to so much of your share?'

'Because I ain't wasted it all on whiskey and wimmin. This silver rush ain't gonna last for ever. I bet Fat Rosie's had most of yourn, ain't she?'

'Not that much.' Pancho made a face. 'A leetle bit. *Sí*, I guess most of eet.'

'Waal,' Tex packed his bundle on to their mule and swung on to the Appaloosa. 'You can stay and give her some more. If you git broke, maybe I'll find you a job on my ranch.'

'Wait a minute, *hombre*. We can get a good price for thees mine.'

'You keep it, Pancho. I gotta git into Oro City, or whatever they call it these days. I said I'd look in at the wedding, so I'll be needin' a hot tub and some new duds. Once she's hitched I'm gittin' outa here.'

'I theenk you fallen for that dame, *amigo*.'

'Waal, she's worked some sorta magic. I cain't git her outa my mind. The only cure's to git far away and fergit her.'

He set the Appaloosa moving at a fast lope down the creek. The clear blue sky against the snowy peaks had a dazzling intensity. It was beautiful country. But somehow he hankered for the plains.

A harmonium was being played gently as friends and well-wishers assembled in the chapel for the wedding of Captain Randall to Careen and Rafael to Lucille. The two sisters looked resplendent in lemon silk dresses, spring flowers entwined in tiaras in their hair, but a tad impatient as the new Holy Joe wittered on: 'My job in this city of sin is to lasso lost souls and bring them into our corral. . . .'

A stranger, tall, with thick blond hair scraped

back across his brow, tastefully attired in a pearl-grey frock coat with satin facings, and black trousers, slipped through the door. 'Have I missed the ceremony?' he asked.

'No, the Bible-thumper's goin' on a bit. They ain't hitched yet,' the usher replied, 'Which side?'

'The bride's.'

'Leave your gunbelt on the hook.'

'I'm not wearing one.' The stranger was carrying a large Bible. 'I've come all the way from Memphis for this.'

He took his seat at the back of the congregation. So, there she was! Older, more full-fleshed, but the same Careen. And there was the old man, her father, with his white mane of hair. He was standing up at the front. The stranger studied them. He twitched his lips with cynical distaste. They would both have to enter the pit of flames. The Klan, their leader, had decreed so.

'Everybody wants to get to Heaven but the trail is long and mighty hard. Too many give up on the way,' the preacher droned on. 'Folks, we gather here today for the wedding of two daughters of our church.'

Guy Lassiter recalled five years of war – how could he ever forget? – slowly retreating to the final surrender at Selma, how he had returned with General Forrest to Memphis, how he had been confronted by his wife's shame.

He opened his hollowed Bible and took out the

revolver and his heart pounded with bitterness and pride in his revenge. He had waited a long time.

Every quarter, officer survivors of The Raiders would meet in a house in Memphis, the room draped with their bullet-holed blood-red flag, now banned, wearing their faded grey uniforms, their decorations, and would hold aloft their long, bloodstained cavalry swords. The Leader would be the last to arrive. His name could not be mentioned. For secrecy he would be wearing a white cloak and conical hood, but how could Guy not recognize the dark eyes smouldering through its slits? He had led them in innumerable cavalry charges against impossible odds, slashing his sabre about him, those eyes flashing his fury. Indeed, once, his horse shot from beneath him, he had jumped up on to the back of Guy's charger and urged him on into battle. To him they had pledged their allegiance, and to the Confederacy, renouncing the loathsome oath forced upon them to the 'united states'.

The Leader had seemed reluctant to raise the name of Careen Lassiter as one who had stained the honour of Southern womanhood, but when he did he intoned, 'Are we agreed the penalty should be death?'

Guy was proud of his reply: 'She has run away, but if she is found I demand the right to carry out execution.'

Aristide Luna rested the barrel of the Omnipotent
on a ledge of the false front to steady his hands. He
had climbed out on to the roof of the two-storey
Timbuctoo Saloon directly opposite the chapel. He
lovingly levered one of the manstopper slugs he had
bought in Denver into the breech ready for firing.
The super-expanding bullets would mushroom on
impact twisting the Texan's insides out, giving him
no chance of recovery. And here he came! Luna
signalled to Luke Short who was standing in a shadowy alleyway on the other side of the street.

Petersen was late, too. He had togged himself
out in a grey tweed suit, blue shirt, loose bow,
shaved and bathed, and was striding across the
mud-hardened main drag to the chapel. Suddenly
he caught sight of the glint of steel, a slight movement on top of the Timbuctoo. Years of living
dangerously made him instinctively duck down on
one knee and pull the Peacemaker .45 from his
holster. Lead snarled whining over his head, nearly
parting his hair and smashed into a horse trough,
shattering it. He raised the heavy revolver at arm's
length and fired without hesitation at the false
front. He could not see the man but a puff of black
powder smoke gave away his position. He rolled
across the ground as the marksman fired again and
a manstopper ploughed into the ground, just missing him. At the back of his mind he thought he

heard the clap of another explosion from behind him. So he moved position again, quickly rolling to one side. He saw the man on the roof more clearly now. He was lining up his sights for another shot. Lying on the ground, the Texan gripped the Peacemaker in both hands, took his time to aim, pulled the trigger.

Up on the roof Aristide stepped out from the false front, the rifle in his hands. He teetered on the edge a few seconds, then pitched forward, hitting the ground on his back. Dead. In the alleyway Short bit his lip, disconcerted by the Texan's tactics. And by Aristide's fall. He had fired one shot from his Hopkins and Allen to no avail as the Texan rolled away.

Petersen climbed to his feet, facing him.

'All right, Luke. Go for it,' he gritted out. Both men snapped off shots fast as dipping swallows. Short bounced back against the alley wall, clutching his shoulder, dropping the .38.

When Tex reached him he was trying to bite back tears of pain. 'Don't kill me,' he begged.

Petersen pointed the smoking Peacemaker at his head. 'If I ever see you again I will, you lousy swash-bucket. So git on your horse, and git outa this town. You're lucky I'm a man of peace.'

He watched the gambler go hobbling away, holding his arm, climb on to a mustang and ride out of town like a canned dog with the denizens of hell on his tail.

'My ma called me Texas 'cause it's the Comanche word for friend,' Tex muttered. 'I guess I'm jest too friendly to these characters.'

'Before I join this young woman, Careen Langridge, in holy matrimony,' the Holy Joe intoned, 'does anyone have any just cause why I should not?'

'Yes.' The stranger stood up, his revolver pointed unerringly at Careen. 'That whore was my wife. She will be no other man's, certainly not some damn Yankee's.'

He turned the gun on the startled Randall, attired in his captain's uniform, with ceremonial sash and sabre, too. He fired and sent the officer crashing back into a stand of bouquets, where he lay, eyes staring, emptily.

Women screamed as Rafael caught hold of Lucille to protect her with his body. None of the men were armed. James Langridge turned, as folks scrambled for cover, and whispered, 'Don't do this, Guy.'

'You are traitors to the sacred cause. You have both been condemned to death.' Guy was relishing this, his blue eyes dilated. He would keep her to the last. 'Die!' His second bullet brought blood flowering through Langridge's shirt. The old man staggered aside, trying to hold on to John Pearce.

The former Confederate smiled and turned the revolver upon Careen, who appeared frozen to the spot, holding her posy of flowers. 'You filthy harlot.'

Hearing the shots Tex went at a run, kicking open the door of the chapel on to a scene of bloody death and confusion. Guy had strode forward towards the pulpit so that at point-blank range he could not miss with his execution of Careen. 'Jezebel! May your soul rot in hell.'

'Hold it!' the Texan shouted, even in such an emergency loath to shoot a man in the back. He clicked back the hammer of the Peacemaker with an easy motion as Guy turned to him, a third bullet blazing from the barrel of his revolver.

'Damn you!' Guy shouted. 'Keep out of it.'

But his aim was flustered. He didn't have a second chance. He stared with disbelief as a bullet kicked into him. 'This bitch needs killing!' He coughed out as, spouting blood, he backpedalled and landed among the flowers on top of the captain.

There was the brimstone reek of drifting gunsmoke as the congregation stood rooted to the spot, staring at three corpses on the floor, their blood oozing out into dark puddles. 'Good Lord,' a woman screeched. 'What a to do. I wasn't expecting this. Thought I was coming to a wedding, not a battle.'

Two days later they gathered by the river for the burials of Langridge and Randall. Guy had been interred without ceremony some distance away.

'Looks like you missed bein' a wealthy widder by

a whisker,' Tex drawled to Careen.

'You're not kidding.' Pale, in black mourning, she sucked in her lips and eyed him. 'The lawyer says the captain had made Raphael his partner, so the mine goes to him. Still, at least Lucille will live in luxury. What are you going to do?'

'Punching cows is what I know, what I'm good at. I'm gonna git me a ranch up in the old Sioux lands.'

'Do you need a squaw?'

He glanced at her and smiled. 'Ranching's a lonely life. I doubt it would be to your taste. There'd be hard times.'

'Aw, hell,' she sighed, 'I've known nothing but hardship and disappointment since the age of thirteen. Let's go for it. I'm willing, if you are.'

'Be sure the damned will find their own hell whatever the cost,' Holy Joe was declaring as the double wedding ceremony began again the next day.

'Hey, preacher, can the fire and brimstone,' Tex butted in. 'Give us a break. This is s'posed to be a happy occasion.'

Don Demetrio and his wife, Eva, had relented of their bitter hatred and come into town after burying Aristide. They wished to give their blessing to their younger son's wedding. Maybe the fact that he'd inherited *their* mine was an incentive. By the time the folks had wished the newly-weds good luck and got stuck into the vittles they had all suddenly become the best of friends.

Aunt Becky had excelled herself preparing a sitdown meal in the new meeting hall, of turkey stuffed with oysters, pecan nuts, raisins, and apricots, with whipped-up potatoes, glazed parsnips and cranberry jelly. It was all as American as the blueberry pie and cream which followed, with applejack brandy or whiskey for the men.

Then they cleared the floor and the fiddles started scraping as a leather-lunged caller growled out, 'Meet your partner and all chaw hay, dozee do an' go away.' High-heeled boots stomped in rhythym as men and women stood in line. Lucille sashayed forward, was swung around by Rafael, and they stepped back. 'Birdie hop out and crane hop in, three hands round an' go it again.'

Careen smiled, radiantly, as she caught hold of Tex when he met her in the centre. He held her tight, leaned her back and drawled, 'The damn licence for you cost me two dollars.'

'The best deal of your life,' she replied, as everybody stomped and clapped.

They parted and it was the turn of the others in the lines to dance up and back, the heftier gals being swung round and round like they were bales of hay, as the caller yelled, 'Hark ye partners, right the same, first lady to the left, do the same again. . . .'

It was a hectic wedding party as the applejack and corn liquor began to take effect. But gradually it quietened down without any trouble and Tex and Careen found themselves swaying in a clinch in the flickering candlelight.

'I guess I've known since that night we were meant to be together,' he murmured, as he felt the softness of her cheek against his jaw, the lilt of her body.

'It's a shame there had to be a tragedy to make me realize that, too.'

'He was a good man, Robbie.'

'Yes.' Careen bit back tears. 'But he was a bit of an old stick-in-the-mud. Very correct. You know, I'm not sure I could have stuck it for long.'

Tex swirled her around and gave a buckaroo yell. 'Strikes me we're just a couple of southern rebels at heart.'

But it was time to extricate themselves from the party, to hug Lucille and Rafael, John and Aunt Becky, shake hands with *Don* Demetrio and Eva, wish them well, and everybody else as they all surged outside to cheer them on the way.

'Come and see us soon,' Lucille cried.

'You come and see us,' Careen replied, as she climbed aboard her chestnut to sit side-saddle. 'We'll only be five hundred miles away.'

Tex swung on to his Appaloosa, and with his baggage mule in tow, went cantering off. 'Come on, gal. We wanna make Cañon City 'fore midnight. Or maybe we'll just sleep under the stars. So long, folks. So long, Leadville.'

'Wait for me!' Careen yipped like a coyote howling for sheer joy as she chased off after him, waving goodbye. 'Montana, here we come,' she cried. 'I hope they're ready for us!'

AUTHOR'S NOTE

This story is mainly a fiction, but based on a factual backdrop. Silver worth $200 million was taken out of Oro City/Leadville's mines by the turn of the century.

Among those who appeared at the famous opera house was Oscar Wilde, who, in 1882, lectured the miners on 'Ethics in Art' and descended the Matchless in an ore bucket.

Luke Short was credited with only two killings, but there may well have been more for he was one of Wyatt Earp's gang when he took over Tombstone. He died, aged 39, of dropsy.

As for billionaire Horace Tabor, he was flat broke by '89 living with his wife and two daughters, one named Silver Dollar, in one room of a hotel in Leadville. He died that year after imploring Baby to 'hang on to the Matchless'.

An eerie ending to his story came in 1935 when the frozen body of an 80-year-old woman was found on the floor of a shack at the deserted ghost mine, the Matchless – it was the once renowned, but by now forgotten, Baby Doe. She had hung on to the flooded mine for nearly half-a-century.